The Whispering Cabin

THE
WHISPERING
CABIN

J. H. Rhodes

AVALON BOOKS
THOMAS BOUREGY AND COMPANY, INC.
NEW YORK

PRINTED IN THE UNITED STATES OF AMERICA
BY HADDON CRAFTSMEN, SCRANTON, PENNSYLVANIA

The Whispering Cabin

CHAPTER ONE

"See, I told you that summer would come, Colleen," Nonie Archers said as the two of them swept through the doors of the grammar school where they both taught.

"I know," Colleen replied as she brushed a strand of her dark-brown hair away from her deep-blue eyes.

Colleen Evans had just completed her first year of teaching, and it had seemed to be both endless and over too soon. "Now I can't believe that I have an entire summer ahead of me. With nothing to do!"

"Both of us," said Nonie, catching her reflection in a school window. She had long ago faced the indisputable fact that Colleen was the beauty of the pair, with her shoulder-length shiny brown hair, her huge eyes, her delicately shaped nose, and her soft, flawless skin.

Nonie, by contrast, was pert and cute, with short-clipped blond hair and a snub nose sprinkled with freckles.

"But you have Terry," said Colleen, referring to Nonie's steady boyfriend, Terry Withers. "It won't seem so long for you."

Nonie cocked her head slightly to look

1

at her best friend. "What about Harold Spears? Haven't you been seeing a lot of him lately?"

"Harold?" Colleen said quietly. "Well, yes, he has taken me out a few times. But I just don't feel the same toward him as you do toward Terry. He's nice and all that...do you know what I'm saying, Nonie?"

Nonie slowly nodded. "Somehow I can't picture you and Harold Spears getting serious. Besides, I think that Harold has a lot of girls that he enjoys seeing. I don't think he's the type to settle for just one girl." She scowled thoughtfully. "Unless he decides he doesn't want anyone *else* going with that girl. Sort of a dog-in-the-manger attitude."

"Do you really think Harold is like that?" Colleen asked. "I guess I just haven't been paying all that much attention to him."

"Well, here he comes now, so you can judge for yourself," Nonie said as a sandy-haired man with a rather florid complexion walked toward them.

"See you later, Colleen," Nonie said. She nodded to Harold, who dismissed her with a quick smile.

"Need a lift home?" he asked Colleen.

"I have my car," replied Colleen as she studied Harold's face, really seeing him for the very first time.

"Good. Say, about tonight," he said, stammering slightly, as though he were trying to decide just how to phrase what he had to say. "I won't be able to take you out. Something else has come up. I'm sorry, but maybe some other time."

Colleen considered Harold thoughtfully and realized that she didn't care a hoot whether he took her to a movie tonight.

"That's all right," she said airily. "A friend of my dad's is coming by and I'd like to meet him. Some other time, Harold."

Before Harold could say anything, Colleen hurried to her car and hopped in. By the time she had driven several blocks away from the school, she had almost forgotten all about Harold Spears. She was suddenly assailed by feelings of restlessness. Even though she had grown up here in this small Minnesota town of Arvin and loved it deeply, Colleen found herself longing to see something else of Minnesota—or anywhere, for that matter.

Oh, she had been to other cities and other states on vacations, but she had never stayed anywhere else for any length of time. Now that summer was here and she was no longer working, it was a perfect time for her to go someplace else. But where?

When she arrived home, her mother was in the kitchen preparing a salad. Colleen brought the mail in and placed it on the table.

"Hi, Mom," she said breezily as she opened the refrigerator and got out some lemonade.

"Hello, dear," Ruth Evans said, smiling at her only child.

Ruth had soft brown hair a shade lighter than her daughter's, but her features were remarkably similar to Colleen's. She was perfectly happy and content to be the wife of Tom Evans, a man she had fallen in love with in high school and married after they both graduated from Arvin High.

"So it's all finished for one year, Colleen. And I see you've survived."

They both laughed. Colleen and her mother had the same sense of humor and saw life in the same optimistic way.

"Even though I enjoyed the past few months, I'm glad the school year's over. Only, now that summer's here..."

Ruth looked at her daughter. "What's wrong dear? Is it anything to do with Harold Spears?"

"Harold Spears?" Colleen said after she had taken a sip of the icy lemonade. "Of course not. At any rate, I don't think it has anything to do with him. It's just that since I don't have to go back to work until September, I was wondering what to do with myself."

"I see," said Ruth, tearing some lettuce leafs apart. "You're just restless and want to see something of the world. Is that a fair assessment?"

"Right as usual, Mom. You know I love Arvin and all that, but..."

Ruth nodded. "It's only natural that you would want to see something of the country. Have you thought about maybe taking a trip?"

"Not really. I know this sounds crazy, but I don't want to just go someplace and then turn around and come back home."

Ruth once more nodded her head.

"You want to go and stay, but you don't know where, is that it?"

"Something like that. I feel kind of up in the air about it."

"Maybe something will turn up. You never can tell what's around the corner." She opened the refrigerator door, then shut it in annoyance. "Oh, dear, I forgot to get butter. And Millard Scott will be here for dinner tonight."

"I'll go to the store and get some," Colleen said, finishing her lemonade. "I take it Millard Scott is the friend that Dad mentioned the other night."

"That's right. Tom met Millard when he was on a business trip years ago. They've been friends ever since. Long-distance friends. But I don't think you've ever met the man. He does have a daughter just your age. That gives the Scotts and us something important in common. Anyway, he's in town for a day or two and Tom has asked him over for dinner."

"He sounds interesting," Colleen said. "I'm looking forward to meeting him."

When Colleen came home with the butter, she saw her father's car parked in the driveway. Next to it was a newer luxury model that she assumed must belong to her father's friend.

Millard Scott turned out to be everything Colleen had pictured him to be and more. His wide, friendly smile was the first thing she noticed, and then his mischievous cobalt-blue eyes.

"And this is Colleen," Tom Evans said proudly as she entered the living room.

"Unbelievable," Millard Scott said. "This is just unbelievable!"

"Why do you say that?" Tom Evans asked. "After all, Colleen was patented after a very lovely model, her mother."

Millard Scott chuckled. "That's not what I meant, Tom. I just can't get over how much my own daughter, Amy, resembles Colleen. You and Ruth never met Amy, did you, Tom? She was away at school or camp the few times you've visited us."

"That's right." Tom Evans turned to his daughter. "I'm sorry, my dear. Colleen, this is my good friend, Millard Scott. But I'm sure you already know that."

"Yes, I assumed as much. Very pleased to meet you, Mr. Scott."

They chatted for a few minutes, and then Ruth Evans rounded them all up for dinner. The conversation and the food were both fabulous, Colleen thought as the evening progressed. Millard Scott was a very interesting man, and he seemed to fit right in with her family.

It was later, when they were all gathered in the den, that Millard brought up the subject of Lake Topaz. "I have this place up there," he was saying, "and Amy had promised to look after it this summer. But something came up, and she had to back out. In the winter, no one would bother the cabin.

But someone should be there in the summer. Yet I can't get away from my business, so the place is just going to sit there without anybody to look after it."

"Where is the cabin?" Colleen asked.

"In the northern part of the state," Millard said. "A good half day's drive or more from Arvin. It's somewhat isolated, but there are neighbors. You couldn't ask for a better place if you're looking for solitude and somewhere to think."

"I see. It sounds wonderful," Colleen said somewhat wistfully.

"Say, what about you, Colleen? How would you like to take care of the place this summer? But I suppose that is out of the question."

"No, it isn't," Ruth Evans said. "Is it, Colleen?"

"Not at all. I really haven't a thing to do this summer," Colleen said. "School is out and I haven't made any plans."

Millard Scott rubbed his hands together. "This is too good to be believed. If you'll take the place, Colleen, I'll pay for your time. It's in good shape. I made some repairs a few weeks ago and stocked up on food. All the utilities are paid for, and the general store will put any groceries on my account."

Colleen agreed that this was too good to be believed.

"What do you say?" Millard asked as he leaned forward in his chair.

"I say that it sounds just wonderful!" Colleen said. "Only, I wouldn't expect to be paid anything for staying there. It's a vacation for me as it is."

Millard insisted that she be paid, and in the end Colleen gave in. He then gave her all the instructions for reaching the town of Lake Topaz and handed her a small key ring with the house keys attached. "Once you're in town, someone can guide you to the cabin. I think you'll enjoy yourself up there. It's very quiet and secluded, as I said before, but Amy managed very well up there last year. Here is a picture of her, by the way."

Millard Scott handed Colleen a snapshot of a girl, and both she and her mother gasped at the same time. "Why, that's you, Colleen!" exclaimed Ruth Evans. "She could pass as your twin sister."

"See what I mean?" Millard said. "That's why I was so overwhelmed when I first saw Colleen."

CHAPTER TWO

It did not take Colleen long to prepare for her unexpected vacation. A few days after she met Millard Scott, she drove into the small town of Lake Topaz. In the distance she thought she saw the sparkle of late-afternoon sunlight on water. It couldn't be far to Millard Scott's summer place now.

Colleen stopped the car in front of a small general store. It seemed as good a spot as any to get detailed directions to the cabin. When she entered the store, she saw a middle-aged man talking to a tall, handsome, broad-shouldered man with copper-colored hair. Colleen guessed his age to be about twenty-eight as his green eyes swept over her from beneath his thick eyebrows. There was a slightly mocking smile on his full lips.

"I'm looking for the Scott cabin," Colleen said to the younger man.

"You must be kidding. You're asking me the directions? Come off it," he said, and Colleen turned from him, feeling the flames rise in her cheeks.

This young man was the rudest person she had ever met. She heard the clomp of his boots as he walked out the door with two bags of groceries, and she hurriedly turned to the older man, who obviously was the owner of the store.

When Colleen explained to him the purpose of her visit, he told her how to find the cabin. Thanking him, Colleen returned to her car.

Before she got in, she caught a glimpse of the rude man once again. He was now leaning against one of the wooden columns of the porch next to the general store. The mocking smile was still on his lips.

As Colleen drove away, she wondered why she had thought he was good-looking. He was the most conceited, obnoxious man she had ever met. And if she ever saw him again, she would tell him as much.

The road that led to Millard Scott's cabin wound its way through some heavily forested land. Occasionally Colleen saw a cabin hidden among the trees. The whole area looked so peaceful, so inviting.

Colleen made a final turn, as instructed, and came upon the cabin. It was built on the slope of a hill. Wooden steps led to a wide porch, and a big garage stood nearby.

Getting out of her car, Colleen rummaged through her purse and found the keys that Millard had given her. She walked up to the door and inserted a key in the lock.

Entering the cabin, Colleen found herself in a living room with a stone fireplace at one end. She crossed the room to an open door, which led to the kitchen.

Colleen wasn't prepared for what she saw now, and a startled scream escaped her lips. The kitchen had been ransacked. Flour and salt or sugar—maybe both—were scattered all over the place.

"What's going on in there?" called a deep, masculine voice from behind Colleen, and she pivoted to see the man who had been so rude to her at the store come striding toward her. "Are you all right, Amy?"

For a moment Colleen was speechless. She just looked at the man, and then her eyes shifted to an oil painting she had seen when she'd first entered the cabin. It hung above the fireplace and its subject was Millard Scott's daughter.

"I'm not Amy," Colleen said when she had found her voice. "My name is Colleen Evans. And just who are you?"

By this time the ruggedly handsome man had crossed the living room and was towering above Colleen. He looked faintly surprised.

"Now that I'm real close, I can see you aren't Amy. But you have to admit the resemblance is uncanny."

"So I've been told. Who are you and what are you doing here?"

"I'm your neighbor, if you're planning on staying here at the cabin. My name is Lincoln Gordon. You may call me Linc. That is, if I'm forgiven for being so rude to you at the general store."

Colleen found it difficult to remain angry

at Lincoln Gordon for very long. She returned the smile that played so easily on his sensual lips.

"Forgiven," Colleen said. "Only, I don't understand why you reacted that way to a stranger."

"I didn't think you were a stranger," Linc said. "I thought that you were Amy Scott and you were playing one of your games."

"Then you know Amy?"

"In a way," Linc said. "We got acquainted last summer when I first moved into my place."

"This is only your second summer here then?"

"That's right. My import-export business on the Coast keeps me busy most of the year. I really look forward to spending a quiet summer here at Lake Topaz."

"Well, my summer isn't starting so quietly," she said, turning from Linc to take another look at the mess in the kitchen.

"No wonder you let out a yell," Linc said, taking a look. "Is this the way you found the kitchen?"

"This is the first time I've been in the cabin," said Colleen. "You don't suppose that Amy left the place like this, do you? Or the men who did some repairs here?"

Linc shook his head as he walked over to the sink. He reached out and tried the window, and it lifted easily at his touch.

"Looks as though some vandal came in here and decided to give you a housewarming," said Linc.

"I think I'd better let the authorities know what went on in here," Colleen said. "Do you know the number of the sheriff's office?"

"Good idea," Linc said. He fumbled in his pockets for a pen and scrap of paper, then wrote the number down for Colleen. "Sheriff Denton should know about this. Only, I think it was probably just somebody's idea of a practical joke."

Colleen glanced around, saw the telephone in the living room, and walked over to dial the number Linc had given her. She waited for a few rings and then, when nobody answered, she hung up.

"He's probably out on his rounds," Linc said. "On the other hand, try again. Give it a few more rings this time."

Again Colleen dialed the number, and just as she was about to hang up a second time, somebody answered on the other end of the line. It was Sheriff Denton. She introduced herself and told him what she had found when she'd entered Millard Scott's cabin.

"I'll be there in a few minutes," Sheriff Denton said. "Are you all alone?"

"No. Mr. Lincoln Gordon is here with me," said Colleen as she glanced across the living room to where Linc was standing.

"Linc there? Have him wait, too," said Sheriff Denton as he hung up.

"He's on his way over," said Colleen. "He asked me to wait here, and you, too."

"As long as we have to wait, I'll go to my car and bring in my thermos of coffee. Would you care for a cup of coffee, Miss Evans?"

"Colleen, please. And that would be wonderful. I'll get some cups, Mr. Gordon."

"That's Linc," Lincoln said as he moved easily across the living room and out the door.

Colleen couldn't help but smile as she hurried to the kitchen for some cups. The more she looked at the mess, the less menacing it appeared. Maybe it was just somebody trying to be funny. Perhaps she had overreacted when she called the sheriff. Still, this wasn't her house, and she felt that Millard Scott would want her to notify the authorities about any kind of break-in.

By the time she had gotten the cups, one extra for the sheriff, and had returned to the living room, Linc was back with the thermos of coffee. As he poured the liquid into two cups, Colleen looked around at the room. One wall was of knotty pine with built-in bookcases and places for what-nots. The stone fireplace was midway along the polished, glistening pine wall. A gray sofa and two overstuffed white chairs were grouped around a glass coffee table. The floor was carpeted, and overall there pervaded a cozy friendliness.

Offering Colleen a cup of the coffee, Linc glanced at the fireplace. "How about a fire? It will take the chill off the cabin."

For the first time, Colleen became aware that the place did have a faint chill to it. Probably because it had been closed up for so long.

"If you don't mind," Colleen said, then took

a sip from the cup.

"My pleasure," Linc said with a slight grin. "Just being neighborly."

Colleen couldn't help but laugh at the way Linc had spoken those words. "Just where do you live, Linc?"

"If you look out that window, you can get a glimpse of it through the trees. It's not as big and fancy as Millard Scott's, but I haven't really begun to add to it yet."

Colleen glanced out the window, but she couldn't see Linc's cabin because it had grown dark outside.

By the time Linc had a blazing fire going in the fireplace, Sheriff Denton arrived. He was a tall, muscular man of about forty-five with a ruddy complexion. When he smiled, he showed big white teeth.

"Have a cup of coffee," Linc offered, tilting the thermos bottle over the third cup.

"Thanks, Linc, don't mind if I do," said the sheriff. Then he turned to Colleen. "You must be the lady who phoned. I'm Sheriff Denton."

"I'm Colleen Evans. As I told you, Millard Scott asked me to look after his cabin for the summer. When I arrived here just a short while ago, I found that somebody had been in the kitchen."

Colleen led the way, with Sheriff Denton and Linc at her heels.

The sheriff made a thorough search of the kitchen, and when he came to the window over the sink, Linc said, "I opened that. It was unlocked."

"Must have been the way they gained ac-

cess to the cabin. Well, I'll look around outside. But I don't think I'll be able to find
anything this evening—it's too dark."

"That's all right, Sheriff Denton," Colleen
said. "I just wanted to report what had happened. It doesn't look as though any real
damage has been done. It's just a big mess
with all the sugar and flour and whatever
strewn about."

Sheriff Denton stayed a little while longer
to finish his coffee. Before he left, he said, "I'll
keep on this, Miss Evans. If I come up with
something, I'll let you know. Let me give you
both my home and office numbers, and don't
be afraid to call me. That's what I'm paid to
do. That is, help people here at Lake Topaz."

After the sheriff had gone, Colleen said,
"He's nice. Like a big, lovable bear."

Linc chuckled. "Better not let him hear
you say that. He thinks he has a reputa-
tion around here for being tough and no-
nonsense."

"I won't tell a soul," Colleen said.

"Well, I think I'd better help you get that
kitchen back into shape. Let me check and
see what we have in the way of cleaning
equipment."

Linc went to a closet and brought out a
couple of brooms, a dustpan, and a mop. He
was very helpful, although Colleen soon realized that he was a little out of his element.

As they worked, Linc kept up a light line of
patter. Colleen felt embarrassed that she had
thought so poorly of the man only a short
time earlier. Still, even though Linc was

being very helpful and neighborly, she wondered why he had so suddenly appeared at her door. It was almost as though he had been expecting her and was waiting for her reaction to the condition of the kitchen.

It didn't take very long to clean up the mess, and Linc volunteered to take the swept-up stuff out to the garbage cans, which were some distance from the cabin. After he had gone, Colleen eyed the kitchen with approval.

Off the kitchen was a small dining area with a table and some chairs. It was separated from the living room by an open partition. Above the table hung wide, oval-shaped lamps.

Going to the refrigerator, Colleen saw that the freezing compartment was full of meat and frozen vegetables, but there was nothing she could defrost in time to fix herself some dinner. She probably should make a quick trip back to the general store to pick up a few things. Closing the refrigerator door, she turned to see Linc coming into the kitchen carrying two bags of groceries.

"What's this?" she asked.

"Sort of a welcome wagon on foot," replied Linc as he put the bags on the table. "I'm inviting myself to dinner. That is, if you can cook steak and make a good salad."

"Of course, I can," laughed Colleen. "I don't know what to say."

"How about, 'How do you like your steak?' That's a good opener."

"You've got yourself a deal," said Colleen.

"Only, I can't accept all these groceries."

"Sure you can," replied Linc as he began to unpack them. "I can afford them, if that's your problem. I'm not on an allowance, as I'm sure you are. Or should I say budget? Anyway, I just drove my car to my place—and I couldn't fit this stuff into my crowded fridge."

Colleen just laughed as she found an apron and tied it around her waist. Linc turned on the transistor radio under some cabinets. Then they talked as she prepared the meal of pan-fried steaks, corn on the cob, and fresh green salad. She found the percolator and got the coffee going so that they could have it with and after their meal.

"This is excellent," Linc said as they sat down to eat. "I'm glad that I stopped by here. If you hadn't screamed, I might never have gotten to know you so quickly."

"So you thought I was Amy Scott," Colleen said.

Linc took a bite of his steak, winked at Colleen, and said, "It's amazing, the resemblance. I'm really not that certain that you aren't Amy, after all, just putting me on about being Colleen."

"Well, I am Colleen, not Amy Scott."

"After taking a bite of this steak, I know for certain you are. Amy was a terrible cook. Besides, you're prettier than she is and your voice is different."

Colleen felt herself blush. To cover her embarrassment, she jumped up from the table and poured a glass of water for each of them.

The flush was a bit less evident by the time she sat down again.

They lingered over their coffee after they had finished eating. Linc said that he would help with the dishes, but Colleen refused.

She told him she would do them in the morning. "Besides, I have to get my things in from the car and unpack."

"I can take a hint," Linc said, getting to his feet. "Remember, Colleen, I live just a short distance away. A short distance as far as the residents here at Lake Topaz are concerned. Call me if you run into any trouble." He wrote down the number for her.

"Let's just hope that our mischief-maker doesn't do an encore," she said.

Linc walked her to her car, then strode off into the darkness. Colleen stood there for a few minutes beside her car, wondering if Lincoln Gordon had really been in the cabin. Or had she imagined it all? The night was suddenly closing in around her, and she heard sounds of animals and insects that were unfamiliar to her.

Colleen made several trips to the cabin with her luggage. Then she parked the car in the garage, closed the cabin's front door, and locked it. She drew the curtains and checked the log in the fireplace. Standing there alone in the living room, Colleen for a moment had a feeling of dread.

The cabin seemed to be whispering all around her.

"That's enough of that, kiddo," Colleen said

aloud, and her voice seemed to dispel what was obviously a fantasy. "You'd better get unpacked and see about making up your bed. You have all summer to start imagining things."

With that dressing down, Colleen went to the master bedroom where she unpacked and found linens for the bed.

She was exhausted when she slipped between the sheets. But as she drifted off to sleep, she once again thought she heard the sound of whispering; yet she was too tired to care or to worry.

CHAPTER THREE

Someone was trying to get into the cabin. Colleen stood in the living room trying to think of a way to get help. The telephone was gone, she didn't know where. And the house seemed to be whispering to her that she was in danger. The whispering grew louder and louder. She put her hands over her ears to drown out the noise, but even that didn't seem to do any good.

Then Colleen saw that one of the windows had been left unlocked; but even as she moved toward it, the window began to move upward. Terrified, she ran to the front door. For some reason she felt that she would be safer outside the house.

It wasn't long before she was lost in the woods. The lower branches of the trees seemed to be eerie, eager hands grabbing at her as she ran along a pathway that was slowly being eaten up by dense undergrowth.

Worse yet, she was being pursued by whoever had tried to get into the cabin. Colleen's breath was coming in quick, painful spurts, and now she was so tired she didn't feel she could go on. It was such an effort to place one foot in front of the other.

She heard the sound of crashing footsteps behind her. Just as her pursuer reached her, Colleen opened her eyes.

"Thank heavens it was just a nightmare!" she said as she frantically cast her gaze around the unfamiliar dark bedroom. She lay there for a few minutes, letting her breathing return to normal before she dared close her eyes and drift off to sleep again.

The next morning when she awoke, the sunlight was streaming into her room, making golden patterns on the bedspread. Flinging the covers away from her body, Colleen got up and put on jeans and a burnt-orange pullover.

She sat for a few minutes in front of the mirror after she had returned from the bathroom, brushing her dark-brown hair until it fairly crackled. Satisfied with her looks, she lightly touched her lips with a glossy lipstick before going into the kitchen.

Colleen made some fresh coffee and then opened the refrigerator. Looking at the eggs, bacon, orange juice, and bread, she suddenly remembered last night and Linc Gordon. And, glancing around, she recalled how the kitchen had looked when she'd first arrived at the cabin. As she reached for the eggs and bacon, she smiled at Linc's thoughtfulness.

Then she turned on the radio and cooked her breakfast. As she ate, she glanced at the window over the sink, the window that Linc had tried and found unlocked last night. Who had left the window like that? Millard Scott, who'd been here a few weeks ago? Or Amy

Scott, who'd been here last summer?

Thinking of Amy, Colleen once again couldn't get over the striking resemblance between them. Looking at that portrait above the fireplace was like looking at a painting of herself. It was truly uncanny.

No wonder Lincoln Gordon had thought she was Amy. The resemblance might turn out to be a problem with other residents here at the lake, too. But didn't Millard Scott say that he had purchased the cabin only two years ago? Or at least Colleen thought he had said as much. So maybe Amy was not that well-known here.

The telephone rang. Colleen got to her feet and hurried into the living room to answer it. It was Sheriff Denton.

"Miss Evans?"

"Yes, speaking."

"I hope that I didn't wake you up."

"Oh, no. I was having breakfast. Do you have some news for me?"

The sheriff hesitated for a moment, then said, "I'm afraid not. I was over there early this morning to check for footprints or any other sort of evidence. I'm afraid I didn't come up with anything that can help."

"That's all right," Colleen said. "It was probably just some harmless mischief-maker."

"Let's hope that's who it was," Sheriff Denton said. "Just don't hesitate to call me if anything else happens there. Lake Topaz has a pretty clean record as far as breaking in and entering is concerned. If this continues, I want to know about it."

Colleen assured him that she wouldn't hesitate to call if there was a problem in the future. "And I do appreciate all that you've done, Sheriff Denton."

"My pleasure. Just hope that you have a pleasant and enjoyable summer here."

After the sheriff had hung up, Colleen went back to the kitchen and finished her breakfast. She didn't know whether to be pleased or not at the information he had given her. Did it mean she would no longer be bothered by vandals? Or did it mean that whoever got into the house was simply clever enough to get rid of any traces that could lead to identification?

"I won't think about it," Colleen said out loud. "After all, I am here to enjoy myself. This is my vacation. And I won't have it ruined."

That seemed to lift her spirits, and she finished her coffee, then attacked the dirty dishes in the sink. When she had completed that job, she decided to give the whole place a once-over. It really wasn't in bad shape, just needed some dusting and vacuuming.

Turning up the volume on the radio, Colleen moved about the cabin, opening windows and letting the sun stream inside. As she dusted the frame on the painting of Amy Scott, she caught herself staring at the girl's features. It was incredible that they should look so much alike. Yet, looking at the painting more carefully, Colleen could see the subtle differences that distinguished her from

Amy. From a distance, however, she saw how easy it would be for anyone to be fooled.

A knock on the front door broke into her thoughts. She rushed to open it.

"Now that's what I call service," Linc Gordon said.

"I was cleaning the cabin and I was just a few steps from the door," she said, feeling a strange trembly sensation at the sight of him.

"Don't want to disturb you," Linc said, starting to turn away.

"You aren't disturbing me," Colleen said, ignoring the weakness in her knees. "Want a cup of coffee? It's freshly made."

Linc smiled warmly. "If it's not too much trouble."

"Come on in," Colleen said. "Everything's in the kitchen. Or do you want me to bring your cup out here to the living room?"

"You lead the way."

Colleen walked briskly to the kitchen, feeling Linc's presence behind her. He took a seat at the table while she poured them both cups of coffee.

"Very good. Hits the spot," Linc said.

"What brings you over here so early in the day?" asked Colleen.

"Just taking my morning walk," said Linc as he gazed at her with guileless eyes. "Saw the windows open and wondered if things were all right."

"Things are fine. Sheriff Denton called a little while ago."

At the mention of the sheriff's name, she

noticed that Linc's eyes narrowed somewhat, but then the look vanished as he said, "Did he have anything to report?"

"You mean about my prowler?"

"Right."

Colleen shook her head. "He didn't find anything that could help. He did tell me I was to call him if I had any further trouble."

"What did he mean by that? Apparently, he doesn't think that this was just the work of some vandal who randomly picked your cabin."

"He didn't say that. Mostly he wanted to reassure me and wish me an enjoyable summer at Lake Topaz."

Linc appeared to be relieved at those words. He slowly took a sip from his coffee and was quiet for a moment or two.

"I hope you have a good time while you're here, also," he finally said. "Normally the area is very peaceful and quiet."

"I certainly hope so," said Colleen with a slight chuckle. "That's one of the reasons I took this place. Although I don't want it to be *too* quiet. If you know what I mean."

Linc grinned. His eyebrow rose slightly. "I believe I do. Well, there is always the lake. We can go boating. That is, if you're interested."

"It sounds like a lot of fun," Colleen quickly replied. "And I am interested. Just think—there's a lake practically in our backyard. You wouldn't find something like that in Arvin."

Linc asked, "Arvin? Where or what is that?"

"It's my hometown," said Colleen. "I'm not surprised that you haven't heard of it. It really isn't very big. But I like it."

"I think I would like it, too," said Linc. "Is that where you work?"

"I'm a schoolteacher there."

"Lucky students."

They both laughed at that, and Colleen found that she was enjoying Lincoln Gordon's company very much.

He finished his coffee, then got to his feet. "I'll be running along. Got work to do. But I'll keep in touch about our ride on the lake."

"Sounds wonderful to me," said Colleen as she walked with Linc to the front door.

After he had gone, all too quickly swallowed up by the dense growth of trees, she returned to her work. Somehow, knowing that Linc was so nearby, Colleen felt safer. But then it occurred to her that it was odd to feel this way. At times while she was talking to Linc in the kitchen, she had been aware of a slight uneasiness—something in the depths of his green eyes that bothered her.

The cabin required more attention than Colleen had originally thought. When she glanced at her watch and saw that it was almost twelve-thirty, she couldn't believe that she had been working all that time.

"You deserve a break," she said aloud, and it sounded like a television commercial. That cheered her up, and she giggled as she went to the kitchen to fix herself a tuna sandwich.

Pouring out the last of the coffee from the percolator, Colleen took her cup and the sandwich out to the front porch. It was a beautiful day, with a slight breeze making it almost chilly where she was sitting. The coffee warmed her, and she munched on her sandwich contentedly.

Just as she was taking her last bite, a middle-aged woman strode up the porch steps.

"So you've come back, Amy," the woman said in a husky voice, running a hand through her long, gray-streaked dark hair. Her thin mouth had a slightly cruel twist to it.

"Oh, you startled me," Colleen said. "You've made a mistake. I'm not Amy Scott. I'm Colleen Evans. Who are you?"

The woman's mouth opened in surprise. "I'm sorry. You do look so much like Amy. But if you say you aren't, then I'll believe you. I'm Ivy Brooks. Live not too far from here."

Colleen felt that Ivy Brooks's unblinking gray eyes were staring right through her. There was something mocking in them. But then she smiled, and the impression fled. She had rather an impish look about her now that belied the harshness Colleen had sensed at first.

"I'm just here for the summer," Colleen said. "First time I've ever lived near a lake."

"It's very quiet here," said Ivy Brooks. "That's why I enjoy it."

"You've been here long, Miss Brooks?"

The woman smiled again. "Ivy, please. And I'll call you Colleen, if that's the name you prefer. Yes, I've come here for what seems ages. Like an old dinosaur."

Colleen smiled at the woman. "You aren't that old. I hope that we'll be friends."

"Of course, we will," Ivy said. "I'll be dropping in now and then. People are very friendly up here. You'll find out."

"I hope I do. I'm already crazy about the scenery. The trees are so beautiful."

Ivy looked around, then back at Colleen. "True. Only, be careful when you take a walk. Easy to get lost here. Anything might happen to you. Well, I'll be seeing you, Colleen. Got to be going now."

Colleen didn't even get a chance to say good-by. Ivy Brooks disappeared around the corner of the cabin so swiftly and silently that it was hard to believe she had ever been there at all.

Still, the warning the woman had given her about the woods echoed in Colleen's ears. It sent a brief, undulating chill down her spine, and she reached for her cup of coffee, hoping it would warm her. It didn't. The chill she was experiencing had nothing to do with the wind or the temperature.

CHAPTER FOUR

"Come on, Colleen," she said aloud. "Only been here one day and already you're getting skittish."

Speaking those words helped her regain her balance. She glanced around at the landscape. Surely there was nothing out there to fear. The trees were beautiful, each one a unique work of art. Oh, yes, there were shadows, but what else could one expect in the woods?

Taking a final sip of coffee, she wondered where Ivy Brooks lived and, for that matter, which cabin belonged to Linc Gordon. She scanned the nearby area. Linc had said that he was her neighbor, so the wooden structure that she could vaguely make out through the trees must belong to him. One of these days she would have to go exploring and see his place up close.

But at the moment she had to get back to cleaning the cabin. She took her cup and plate and went inside.

When everything was spick-and-span, and Colleen had become acquainted with all the rooms and closets, she telephoned her mother.

Ruth Evans was excited at hearing her daughter's voice. "Oh, Colleen, are you all right? Did you have a safe trip?"

"Yes, Mom, everything went very smoothly. I didn't have any problems with the car at all. And I've been spending my first day cleaning up the cabin."

"Is it a nice place?"

"Very," Colleen said. "It has everything. Much more than one person needs. Two bedrooms, a big kitchen, living room, dining room, the works. And nicely furnished. I think that you would really enjoy seeing the cabin."

"Maybe next year I can talk your father into taking me up to Lake Topaz for a vacation. Of course, you'll have to come along, too, since you'll know all about the place by that time. Anything interesting happen? Have you met anybody?"

Colleen paused a moment before she spoke. She didn't think that she should tell her mother about the condition she had found the kitchen in when she arrived. There was no point in worrying her.

"Well, I've met my nearest neighbor, a man named Lincoln Gordon. He seems very nice. And today a woman, Ivy Brooks, came by and chatted with me. People seem to be very friendly up here."

"That's nice, dear. Oh, Nonie is here visiting. I'll put her on. That'll give me time to fix her and me my sinful sundae concoction and coffee. You probably have a lot of things to tell her. Take good care of yourself, dear. And enjoy your vacation."

Colleen's best friend got on the phone. "What's this about your meeting some people up there? Who are they? One of them a man?"

Colleen laughed. "As a matter of fact, you're right, Nonie. His name is Lincoln Gordon."

"Sounds romantic. How old is he and what does he look like?"

Colleen described Linc as best she could, and she found that just saying his name gave her that weak feeling in her knees that she had experienced before.

"How did you meet?"

Colleen told Nonie about the episode in the general store and about finding the mess in the kitchen when she first arrived and how her neighbor had helped her clean things up. "But please don't tell Mom about it, okay?"

"Okay. But tell me more."

"Well, I guess someone got into the cabin through an unlocked window. I think it was just some kid trying to be funny. Nothing to worry about. I did call the sheriff, though."

"What did he do?"

"Sheriff Denton was very nice and looked around. He didn't come up with anything. Since nothing was really damaged—and I doubt there was anything valuable to steal— well, like I said, there's nothing to worry about. Besides, the sheriff isn't very far away, and Linc isn't, either."

"Oh, so it's Linc, is it?" Nonie teased. "That sounds serious."

"He's just a neighbor," Colleen replied, happy that Nonie couldn't see the flush that was now on her face.

"Well, I hope you have a good time while you're there, Colleen," Nonie said. "Only, what happened in the kitchen makes me feel kind of creepy."

"Sheriff Denton didn't think it was anything to be alarmed about. Whoever got into the house apparently didn't take anything, as I said. Or at least I don't think so."

There was an uneasy pause at the other end of the line. "Are you sure you want to stay there alone, Colleen? You know I could get away and come up there for a few days anyway."

"Of course, I'm not afraid to stay alone. I guess I shouldn't have told you about the kitchen episode."

"I'm glad you did. If you don't want me to come, at least be careful and keep a sharp eye out for anything unusual while you're there."

"Don't worry, Nonie, I will," Colleen said, and then she switched the topic of conversation to Terry Withers.

That kept Nonie busy talking and took Colleen's thoughts away from Lake Topaz. When Colleen finally hung up, she was feeling much better.

Going into the kitchen she checked the refrigerator. In spite of Linc's generous gift of groceries the night before, Colleen needed to go to the general store.

Glancing around to make certain that all the windows were securely locked, she took her purse and left the cabin. It was a short drive to the store.

The owner, who had given her directions yesterday, remembered her and said, "Found the cabin all right, I see."

Colleen noticed that several customers were listening as she said, "Yes, thanks. I need a few things. Do I just help myself?"

The man smiled and nodded. "You're staying at the Scott cabin for the summer, right?"

"That's right."

"Mr. Scott called and okayed your credit. You don't pay for a thing when you shop here, Miss Evans."

Colleen smiled weakly as she thanked him. Even though she appreciated what Millard Scott had done, she felt peculiar because most of the customers now knew where she was staying and what her name was.

While she was filling her cart, a girl came up and said, "Amy?" When Colleen looked directly at her, she said, "I'm sorry. You look so much like someone I know."

"I seem to be getting that everywhere I go around here," said Colleen, and then she smiled at the girl, who returned the smile before walking away.

Colleen was surprised at the fine quality of the food in the general store, and she told the owner as much while he bagged her groceries.

"Got quite a colony of people living up here

in the summer," he said. "Oh, you can't see all the houses. They're pretty well concealed by the trees. But there are enough folks so I have to have good stuff—and some fancy things—on my shelves and in the meat counter."

Colleen thought about what he had said as she drove back to the cabin. So a lot of other cabins were hidden away behind the protection of the trees. Sure enough, every once in a while she caught a glimpse of one as she drove toward the Scott place.

As she neared the turnoff to the cabin, she saw a familiar figure walking along the road, and she touched the brake. It was Lincoln Gordon. A wry smile curved his lips when he saw her.

"Twice in one day," Linc said. "This really more than makes my day."

"Would you like to try for three times?" Colleen said, brushing a strand of dark-brown hair out of her eyes. "I'm fixing chicken cacciatore for supper. Would you like to join me? Sort of a small repayment for your helping me out yesterday."

Linc's smile deepened. "You don't have to repay me, but I accept. Chicken cacciatore is one of my favorite dishes. How did you know that?"

"Just a lucky guess," Colleen said. She took her foot off the brake and the car began to move slowly away from him. "See you around six-thirty, okay?"

He made an okay sign with his hand as Colleen drove away.

When she reached the cabin, she checked it over to make sure it was all tidy. In one of the closets she even found two colorful throw rugs that she put on the porch. Then Colleen started the dinner, showered, and put on some fresh slacks and a blue knit shirt.

She had just finished setting the table when Linc knocked on the door. He looked ruggedly handsome in his denim jacket, burgundy shirt, and blue corduroy pants.

"Smells wonderful," Linc said, taking off his jacket and putting it on a living-room chair. "I've been looking forward to this meal all afternoon."

"Hope you aren't disappointed."

"After last night, I don't think there's a chance."

Colleen led him into the dining room where the food was waiting. She had to admit to herself that this really was the best chicken she had prepared in her entire life. Or it seemed that way.

Linc was a witty and clever dinner companion with a wealth of stories to tell. They decided to take a walk after eating, but first Linc helped Colleen with the dishes.

As they left the cabin, he said, "You should go into the catering business. That was delicious. Or are you used to people telling you things like that?"

"If I were, which I'm not, I don't think I'd tire of it soon."

It was dark as they walked along the narrow path that led away from the cabin. The moon overhead sent its beams down through the branches of the trees.

They were both contented, and conversation didn't seem necessary. At one point Linc paused to examine something he had found on the ground. Colleen continued on, thinking he would catch up with her.

Suddenly a noise in the underbrush startled her, and she paused to glance around. She was all alone in the woods. Linc was nowhere to be seen. The noise that had disturbed her grew louder, and all at once an old man with big eyeglasses and a bushy white beard jumped out of the greenery.

It was so unexpected that Colleen screamed.

"No need to holler like that, young woman," the newcomer rasped. "Why, you'll wake every sleeping body from Lake Topaz to Minneapolis."

At that moment Linc came rushing around a bend in the path. "What's wrong, Colleen?" He turned to the old man. "Oh, hi, Scags."

"I'm sorry," Colleen said. "It was foolish of me to scream like that."

"What she means, Linc, is that I scared her," the old man said. "And I apologize for that, young lady."

"Colleen, this is Scags Barnett," Linc said. "Our local character. Also one of our nicest citizens."

"Hello, Mr. Barnett," Colleen said, lowering her head slightly in embarrassment.

"Scags, it is. And you're going to be Colleen to me," said the old man. "Now that the amenities are over and done with, why don't you two buy me a cup of hot coffee?"

"I forgot to tell you," Linc said as he took Colleen's arm. "Scags is also the biggest moocher on the lake."

"But I have style," Scags said brightly. "You've got to admit that."

Colleen allowed herself to be led by Linc toward a turnoff that would take them to town, Scags following in their wake.

CHAPTER FIVE

Linc took Colleen and Scags to a small restaurant in Lake Topaz. There was a friendly atmosphere to the place, as though everyone there knew everyone else. The waitress, a woman in her late forties, came over to greet them.

"Well, Lincoln Gordon, I thought you knew better than to be found in the company of Scags Barnett," she said in a mock-serious way. "Although I can see that you at least showed some good taste as far as this girl is concerned."

"Roxie, this is Colleen Evans. Colleen, this is Roxie," Linc said. "She's sassy and talks too much, but she's the best waitress at Lake Topaz."

Colleen and Roxie exchanged greetings. Colleen immediately liked the rather raucous older woman. Even though Roxie kidded Scags Barnett, who was clearly not at a loss for comebacks, she was obviously quite fond of the eccentric old man.

When they had taken seats at a table near one of the windows, Roxie brought them all hot, steaming mugs of coffee. She also brought over some small sweet rolls that tasted as though they were homemade.

"Best coffee in these parts," said Scags as he lifted his mug to his lips. "Even if it is served by Roxie."

Colleen searched the old man's face and saw that he was just joking. There was a faint twinkle in Scags's eyes that told her he secretly enjoyed sparring with Roxie.

After they had settled down to enjoying the rolls and the coffee, Linc said, "What are you doing wandering around on a night like this, Scags?"

"What's wrong with tonight?" the old man said, somewhat defiantly. "Anyhow, I was just enjoying the night air."

Linc turned to Colleen. "Scags goes way back, as far as Lake Topaz is concerned. He can tell you stories about the place you wouldn't believe."

"And all of 'em is true," said Scags proudly. "I can remember back when there wasn't but a handful of cabins up here. And we didn't have roads in those days, just wide paths. Can't say that progress is all that great. Sure was a lot quieter in those days."

Colleen couldn't imagine a quieter place than Lake Topaz was last night—or tonight, for that matter. And she said as much.

"Maybe that's because you're from a place that is noisy, Colleen," Scags said not unkindly. "I can remember when you could hear a person whisper from across the lake. You could hear 'em plain as day on this side of the water. Now that's what I mean when I say quiet."

"Come on, Scags," said Linc. "You don't expect us to believe that, do you?"

"Of course, I do," Scags said, momentarily assuming a hurt expression. "Well, let's just say that it was a lot quieter around these parts then than it is now."

"Where do you live, Scags?" Colleen asked. "I mean, is your cabin very far from here?"

Scags smiled at Colleen. He looked a little bit like Santa Claus when he smiled, Colleen thought.

"Not too far, young lady," he said. "I remember once we all got snowed in here—a few of us live here all year—and I was having people over for my famous Irish stew. Nobody could go home for three days. It was a good thing I made a lot of stew!"

Colleen and Linc both laughed, although Colleen wondered just how much truth lay in Scags's stories. He had a way of mixing reality with fantasy that made it difficult to discern which was which.

"Lots of stories go with Lake Topaz," Scags went on. "Like the one about all the money that's supposed to be hidden at the Scott cabin."

Colleen suddenly sobered. For an instant the memory of what she had found in the kitchen on her arrival at the cabin came rushing back to her.

But she pushed the unwelcome thought out of her mind as she asked, "What money are you talking about, Scags? And where is it supposed to be hidden?"

Noticing the old man's coffee mug was

empty, Linc motioned to Roxie, who came hurrying over with a refill.

"There, that ought to hold you for about three more of your tall tales," Roxie said, then walked away.

"Someday I'll have the right comeback to make to that remark," Scags said, lifting his mug to his lips. He tasted the coffee, and a wide smile spread across his face. "Still, she serves the best coffee in these parts."

"Okay, Scags," said Linc. "Quit procrastinating. You know that Colleen and I are dying to hear what you have to say about the Scott cabin and the money."

"Oh, that," Scags said, enjoying his little bit of theatrics. "Well, it wasn't the Scott place then. It belonged to Walter Banning. Mr. Scott bought it from Walt, or rather from his widow."

Colleen stole a glance at Linc, who looked as exasperated as she felt. Apparently there was no way that a person could hurry Scags Barnett if he didn't want to be hurried. So she just sat back and waited.

"Anyway, back then when it happened, the place was empty and it belonged to Walt Banning. It was the craziest scheme you ever heard of. Mel Branson—he was the one who stole the money in the first place—parachuted out of an airplane and landed here at the lake with his satchel of stolen money."

"Mel Branson," Linc said thoughtfully. "I think I read something about him in the papers not too long ago. Didn't he die in prison?"

"That's right," Colleen said. "He was supposed to have held up a bank and made off with hundreds of thousands of dollars. Only, the money was never found."

Scags smiled knowingly. "So they say. But they caught Mel Branson right here in Lake Topaz. And he didn't have the money on him. They also found that he had broken into the Scott cabin and had hidden there for a few days."

Colleen looked askance at Linc, a smile on discern whether this was really the truth or just another of his stories designed to fool greenhorns like herself.

"You mean, Scags, that nobody has found that money yet?" asked Colleen as she reached for her coffee once again.

"So I heard."

Colleen looked askance at Linc, a smile on her lips, but she was surprised to see that he was looking at Scags with a deadly intensity.

When Linc noticed that Colleen was looking at him, he relaxed and smiled, but Colleen found it difficult to forget that look of grim concentration.

"That's a good story, Scags," Linc said in a lighthearted way. "Only, I would think by this time somebody would have found all that money if it was ever really there."

"Oh, they found a little of it," said Scags. "It was on Mel Branson when the police picked him up. Big mistake on his part. Otherwise, they might not have had a case against him."

At this point Roxie came back with her pot

of coffee. "Refill, folks?"

Simultaneously everybody nodded.

"What you up to, Scags?" Roxie asked. "Looks to me like you've been telling some more of your tall tales to these people. Which one was it this time?"

Scags looked wounded at Roxie's remark. "I don't tell tales, as you put it. I was just informing these people about Mel Branson, the bank robber."

Roxie poured some coffee into Scags's mug and then said, "I kind of like that one myself."

Having said this, Roxie turned and walked away to another table.

"Don't take it so hard, Scags," Linc said. "Colleen and I believe what you told us. Just think, if someone found that money, well..."

"I know what you're saying, Linc," replied Scags. "Only, the authorities went over that cabin with a fine-toothed comb. They couldn't find a trace of the money. So it still must be in the cabin, only hidden so well that nobody will ever spot it."

Linc took a sip of his coffee and said, "Who knows? Maybe it will be found someday."

"Do you think that Mr. Scott knows about the money?" asked Colleen.

"Probably," said Scags. "I'm not the only one who knows that story up here at the lake. It's still quite a conversation piece. And people around these parts still speculate as to where Mel Branson hid his loot."

Colleen shook her head. "This sounds like something out of a mystery novel. I wonder if this Mel Branson ever told anyone where the money was hidden. I mean, before he died."

Scags shrugged. "No way of telling. Only, I kind of doubt that he would do that. Probably thought he had put the money in a safe place and would come for it when he either got released or escaped from prison. Only, it didn't happen that way for him."

"Then you really are convinced that the money from the bank robbery is still in the cabin that Colleen is staying at?" asked Linc.

"Nobody had convinced me otherwise," was Scags's reply as he reached for the last of the rolls.

Colleen looked at the old man and thought again about the condition she had found the kitchen in when she had arrived at the Scott cabin. Had the intruder been looking for the money? If that was the case, then why leave such a mess with the flour and such?

It might have been done to cover up the actual motive for entering the cabin, Colleen thought as she tried to direct her attention once again to Linc and Scags. But it seemed pretty farfetched, the idea that someone would go to all that trouble just to allay suspicion.

"Penny for your thoughts?" Linc said to Colleen.

"Oh, nothing really important."

"Has it anything to do with the way you found the cabin when you arrived?" asked Linc.

"Something like that," Colleen replied.

"Only, Sheriff Denton didn't mention anything to me about being suspicious of someone looking for stolen money that's supposed to be in the cabin."

"He probably didn't want to alarm you," Linc said.

After that they talked of other things. Scags had a wealth of stories to tell and Roxie kept stopping by to kid him or add a little to the story he happened to be relating.

Colleen found that she was thoroughly enjoying herself. This was the way she had imagined her vacation would be. Occasionally someone new entered the small restaurant and, since Scags knew everyone at Lake Topaz, the newcomer usually stopped at their table for a brief chat. Colleen knew that by tomorrow morning she wouldn't be able to remember any of their names. But it was interesting to meet so many new people.

Scags Barnett finally got to his feet and told everyone that he was going home. "It's not the late hour or the company," he said. "It's just that I have something to do at home."

Linc told him to be careful going home, but Scags ignored the warning. He said, "I've been living here longer than the bears. I can find my way home blindfolded."

Roxie tried to talk Scags into taking a flashlight with him, but he refused.

"He's too independent for his own good," Roxie said after the old man had left the restaurant.

"I hope he'll be all right," Colleen said anxiously.

Roxie patted her on the shoulder. "Don't worry about him, honey. Scags knows his way around here better than anyone else. Even though he is getting older."

Colleen glanced at her watch. "I think I'd better get going, too. I didn't realize it was getting this late."

Linc got to his feet. "I'll walk with you. Seeing as how that was the way we started the evening off. That is, before we met Scags Barnett."

"You can stay if you like," Colleen said. "I think I'll be able to find my way back to the cabin. If Scags can do it, then so can I."

Linc shook his head as he left some money on the table to pay their bill. "You aren't Scags. And I'm glad of that."

When they began walking out of town, Colleen said, "That was fun."

"Well, I'm glad you enjoyed yourself. We'll do it again sometime."

They chatted all the way up the road and along the path that led to her cabin.

When they were within sight of the place, Colleen said, "I can make it from here, Linc. Thanks for being so gallant."

Linc lightly touched his forehead with his hand and said, "My pleasure, Miss Colleen. But I can walk all the way with you if you like."

Colleen told him it wasn't necessary since it was such a short distance, and then Linc said good night. As Colleen turned to glance down the path, she saw that Linc had already been swallowed up by the dark night.

Feeling somewhat strange, now that she was alone, Colleen quickened her stride until she reached the porch steps. When she was on the top step, she thought she saw a movement.

In the next instant, something was suddenly thrown over her head, and she was pushed down the stairs.

CHAPTER SIX

Colleen was stunned but not hurt. She flung whatever was over her face away and sat up. Whoever had been on the porch had used one of the throw rugs to catch her off balance. Then the person had pushed her down the stairs. Instead of feeling fright, Colleen felt anger.

She got to her feet and stood staring up at the shadowy darkness of the porch. Whoever had done this to her might still be around.

Then she saw a flicker from a flashlight behind her being focused on the porch. She pivoted and saw someone approaching with the flashlight.

"Are you all right?" came a voice from behind the light that was now being beamed on Colleen.

She threw up a shielding arm to ward off the brightness. "Yes, but please don't shine that thing in my eyes."

"Sorry," came the masculine voice in the darkness. "I was just out for a walk when I heard a noise over here and I came to investigate. What's going on?"

Colleen wasn't at all certain that she wanted to discuss this with a perfect stranger. But, as she had learned that evening, people got acquainted quite quickly here at Lake Topaz.

"Oh, things are all right now," Colleen said, not allowing herself to give way to her emotions.

"Are they? I'm Jason Lewis. Don't think I've seen you before. Are you just visiting the lake?"

Colleen by this time could make out the stranger's face. The moon had come out from behind a cloud and its brilliance lighted up the area where they stood.

Jason Lewis had dark, wavy hair that was clipped short. She couldn't be certain, but he appeared to have brown eyes with dark, full eyebrows. Though his nose was a little too long, his overall appearance was attractive.

"You might say that I'm visiting. I'm here for the summer, taking care of Millard Scott's cabin. I'm Colleen Evans."

"Now that the formalities are over and done with," Jason said, "how about telling me what's been going on here? Or am I being a busybody?"

By this time Colleen had decided that Jason Lewis meant her no harm, and he did appear to be genuinely interested in her welfare.

"Not in the least. To tell you the truth, I'm really not certain just what did happen when I walked back here from the restaurant."

"You were out walking alone?"

Colleen shook her head. "No, somebody was with me. He left me a little way back from the cabin. It was my idea."

"I see. Please go on."

"Anyway, when I got here, I started up the steps. When I got to the top, I felt that someone was there. Before I could look around, something was suddenly thrown over my head and I was pushed backward."

Jason flashed the light around until he spotted the throw rug. "This must have been what they used."

"It was. There are two of those on the front porch."

"Any idea who might have done this?"

"Not in the least," she said.

"You didn't get any kind of look at the person?"

Once again Colleen shook her head. "It was too dark. Besides, as I said, it was so sudden and I wasn't expecting anything like that."

"You didn't injure yourself when you fell?"

"Just my pride," Colleen said.

Jason chuckled. It was an infectious laugh and Colleen found that she was joining in with him, even though what had happened to her was very serious.

"But really, you have no idea who it might have been?" asked Jason again, his voice taking on a more serious tone.

"I've only been here two days," replied Colleen. "It could have been just about anyone. Sheriff Denton seemed to think the last incident was just caused by a vandal who broke into the cabin."

"The last incident! You mean something else happened to you?"

"Yes, and I think I'd better call the sheriff right away. He told me to if anything else happened."

Colleen wasn't surprised that Jason Lewis followed her into the cabin. After all, wasn't that the way things were done here at Lake Topaz? Or, anyway, it seemed that way. People never considered themselves strangers.

When they entered the living room, Colleen switched on the light.

"Amy, it's you!" Jason gasped. "But it can't be!"

With a quick glance at the portrait above the fireplace, Colleen shook her head. "No, I'm me and that's Amy. Only, I'm finding it harder and harder to convince people that I'm who I say I am."

"It's incredible," Jason said in wonderment. "The resemblance is uncanny. Are you sure you aren't Amy Scott?"

"Positive," replied Colleen with a touch of irritation. "I think I should know who I am, Mr. Lewis."

Colleen's suddenly formal tone made Jason wince. "Please, I'll make a deal with you. If you'll let me call you Colleen, then I'll feel more at ease if you refer to me as Jason. I have a feeling that we're going to see a lot of each other this summer, so there isn't any real reason for us to be so formal."

"You seem very sure of yourself."

There was a smug smile on Jason's lips. "Of course. I'm a very positive person. I have a great deal to be positive about. And you will come to realize that after you get to know me."

"I'll think about that," Colleen said as she reached for the telephone. "In the meantime, I have to call the sheriff. Do you want to stick around for a cup of coffee, Jason?"

"Wild stallions couldn't drag me away from an offer like that."

Once again Jason chuckled, but Colleen fought the desire to join him. She didn't think amusement was what she wanted to convey in her call to Sheriff Denton.

When he answered, Colleen quickly told him what had happened after she had returned from the restaurant.

"Are you all right?" Sheriff Denton asked. "Did you hurt yourself in the fall?"

"I'm fine, really I am. I didn't hurt myself at all," Colleen said. "And that makes me feel lucky. Jason Lewis happened to be coming by the cabin at the time and he came to my rescue."

"Jason Lewis, huh? Do you know the man?"

"Never met him until tonight. Anyway, he's with me right now. I thought I'd fix us some coffee."

"I'll be right over," Sheriff Denton said. "Maybe I can find some trace of whoever did this to you. Although a really thorough going-over many have to wait for daylight."

"I'll save you a cup of coffee, Sheriff," Colleen said.

After she hung up, she turned to face Jason

Lewis, who had been staring at her all the time she had been talking to the sheriff.

"So the minion of the law is on his way over here," Jason said.

"He wanted to see if he could find some clue as to who attacked me."

"At this hour?"

"Sheriff Denton apparently doesn't think it's too late."

Colleen hurried to the kitchen where she found a nearly full pot of coffee still plugged in. Pouring two cups, she took them into the living room.

"Thanks," Jason said as she handed him a cup. "This should hit the spot on a night like this."

"What sort of work do you do at the lake?" asked Colleen out of curiosity, sensing he was not just another vacationer.

"I own the marina," Jason said. "And I own a few cabins in the area that I rent out. You'll have to come over to the marina someday and let me take you for a ride on the lake."

"Sounds like a wonderful idea," replied Colleen. "I'd like to see as much of Lake Topaz as I can while I'm here."

"Are you related to Millard Scott?"

Colleen shook her head. "But my father is a good friend of his. It was Mr. Scott who suggested I come here for the summer. He didn't have anyone to look after the cabin, and since my work was over for the year, I decided to take him up on his offer."

"So you're probably a poor teacher, right? I

bet those difficult students can hardly wait to
get to school," Jason said, and a slight leer
touched his lips.

"So far I like my work," said Colleen. "And
I haven't run into any difficult children."

"Are you from a small town?"

Jason Lewis certainly was direct when he
asked a question, Colleen thought. But she
found that she was telling him all about her
hometown and her parents and even her
best friend, Nonie.

"Very interesting indeed," was Jason's
comment when she finished, although Colleen had the impression that Jason really
wasn't all that interested in where she came
from and who her friends were. "You haven't
mentioned a steady boyfriend. Surely someone with your looks isn't without an admirer?"

Colleen couldn't decide whether Jason's
old-fashioned phrasing of the question was
meant to be playful or serious.

"Oh, I have an admirer, as you put it,"
Colleen said, "but I'm not sure how much I
admire him."

She wasn't certain but Jason appeared to
breathe a sigh of relief at her words.

"Too bad. Arvin doesn't sound as though it
deserves to have you living there."

It was a compliment, and Colleen felt the
color rush to her cheeks. Before she could say
anything more, there was a quick rap at the
door. She hurried to answer it, happy for the
interruption.

"Please come in, Sheriff," Colleen said. "I don't know whether you know Jason Lewis or not."

"We've met," Sheriff Denton said in an expressionless voice.

"That's right," said Jason. "I'd better run along. I'm sure the sheriff has many questions to ask you, Colleen. Think over what I said about coming to the marina. I think I can show you a very interesting time."

"I will," said Colleen as Jason walked briskly past her and out into the night. She got a quick impression that he was not very happy to see the sheriff and vice versa. Or was she only imagining it because she was upset by the porch incident?

After she had poured the sheriff a cup of coffee, she quickly explained once again what had happened to her after she had returned to the cabin that night.

"And you didn't get a good look at whoever did it?"

"I have no idea who it might be."

"Let me take a look around out there," Sheriff Denton said as he put down his cup of coffee. "Would you mind coming with me and showing me where it happened?"

Colleen showed the sheriff exactly where she had been standing when attacked, and he spent some time looking around the area. When he finally finished, he told her that he would check again in the morning.

After he had gone, Colleen locked up the place and rinsed out the cups. Going to her room, she put on her pajamas and climbed into bed. She was too keyed up to sleep, so she just lay there looking at the ceiling with the light on, trying to beckon drowsiness.

Instead of getting sleepy, she found herself thinking of Lincoln Gordon. Was it possible that he might have been the one who had tossed the rug over her head and pushed her down the stairs? He could easily have circled back and crept onto the porch before she got there. Only, she didn't want to believe that Linc Gordon would do such a thing.

Or it might have been Jason Lewis. After all, she had just taken his word that he had been out walking and had heard a noise. And what about Scags Barnett?...

Before Colleen could pursue that train of thought, she heard a sound from outside the cabin. It seemed to come from the front porch.

Grabbing her robe, Colleen hurried to the living room where she picked up a piece of firewood before opening the front door.

Cautiously she stuck her head out and looked around. She didn't see anyone on the porch, and all she could hear was the sighing of the wind through the pine trees. Feeling braver, Colleen stepped out the door and onto the porch.

She still clutched the piece of firewood in her hand and this added to her boldness. She stood there listening for a brief time, but she could not hear anything that would indicate someone had been on the porch.

Deciding it must have been her imagination, she walked back inside and locked the door. Dropping the piece of firewood into its metal container near the fireplace, she went back to her bedroom.

Slipping once again into bed, Colleen drifted off to sleep. Her dreams that night were plagued by shadowy creatures who attempted to get into the cabin through the windows and doors, through the floor and the fireplace.

CHAPTER SEVEN

The next morning, after Colleen took a cold, bracing shower, she dressed in jeans and a loose-fitting shirt. She put on her jogging shoes for comfort, then headed for the kitchen. Making a fresh pot of coffee, she scrambled an egg and toasted an English muffin.

Colleen parted the curtains above the kitchen sink and glanced out at the morning. She saw a movement outside the window and for a moment she was startled. Then she recognized the stocky build of Sheriff Denton, and she sighed with relief as she took her food to the table.

Colleen had just finished her breakfast and was pouring herself a second cup of coffee when the sheriff rapped lightly on the kitchen door.

"I thought you might be up," he said in a friendly tone. "I smelled the coffee all the way outside."

"Please come in, Sheriff," Colleen said. "Would you care for a cup of coffee? I always make plenty."

"If it's not too much trouble."

"Not in the least," Colleen said as she got

out a cup and filled it with the hot liquid.

"Thanks." He sipped the coffee, then leaned against the counter. "I was up here checking to see if I could find anything about your attacker."

"Any luck?"

Sheriff Denton shook his head. "Oh, there were some bushes bent over, but I couldn't find any clear footprints. I haven't so far been able to come up with anything that can help me. You haven't any idea who this person might be?"

"No, I haven't," Colleen sighed. "Although I've been thinking over what I heard at the restaurant last night. Do you know a man named Scags Barnett?"

A slight chuckle escaped Sheriff Denton's lips. "Yes, I know old Scags. He's quite a character. Been here at Lake Topaz for years. Why do you ask?"

"Oh, I don't suspect Scags of doing this. It's just that he was telling us a story last night."

"Us?"

"Lincoln Gordon and myself."

"Go on."

Colleen paused long enough to take a quick, bracing sip from her cup. "Well, he told us about a criminal who had stolen some money and left it here at the cabin, or some-where nearby."

Sheriff Denton again chuckled. "Old Scags is full of stories. I wouldn't pay too much attention to his fanciful tales."

"You mean there really wasn't a man named Mel Branson?"

"Oh, Branson is real, all right. But just because the money was never found doesn't mean that he left it in this cabin. He was in the area for a few days before he was discovered. Branson could have hidden the money anyplace."

"Then you don't believe the money is still here?"

Sheriff Denton was thoughtful for a moment and then said, "I really don't know, Miss Evans. Do you think that perhaps the stolen money has something to do with what's been happening here at the cabin?"

"It might," Colleen said lightly. "Of course, it's just a theory."

"Worth considering," said the sheriff as he finished his coffee. "If I come up with anything else, I'll let you know, Miss Evans. And, remember, call me if you have any other problems here at the cabin."

"I will."

Before the sheriff walked out of the kitchen, he paused and said, "You make a good cup of coffee. Thanks again."

Colleen nodded as the stocky man left. At that moment the telephone rang and she hurried into the living room to answer it.

"Didn't get you out of bed, did I?" Linc Gordon asked.

"Oh, no. I've been up for hours. Sheriff Denton was just here."

"A social visit?"

"No, business. Seems I had a visitor last night. When I got to the cabin, someone threw a rug from the porch over my head and pushed me down the stairs."

There was a brief silence on the other end of the connection, and then Linc said, "Are you all right, Colleen? You weren't hurt?"

"No, I'm fine. Whoever did it just pushed me down and then ran away."

"You have any idea who did it? Did you see anyone?"

"I'm afraid I didn't. That's why I called the sheriff last night. He came over and looked around and then returned this morning. He wasn't able to come up with anything."

"I see. Well, that just makes my call more urgent. I thought you might like to go on a picnic this afternoon, have a look at the scenery. I'm a very good guide."

"A picnic! That sounds wonderful," said Colleen with enthusiasm. "When?"

"How about one o'clock? Is that too soon?"

"Sounds fine to me. Can I fix anything?"

There was a faint, mocking laugh at the other end of the connection. "This is my picnic and I'll take care of the food. And the entertainment."

"I'll see you at one o'clock," Colleen said as she replaced the phone in its cradle. She glanced at her watch. It would be a while before Linc came by, so she had time to do some reading and possibly write some letters.

First, however, she walked out to the front porch to look around. Perhaps she might see something that the sheriff had overlooked. Walking the length of the porch, Colleen cautiously and carefully examined every square inch of it. She didn't know what she was looking for, and therefore she gave up after she had walked the entire length three times.

As she started back to the front door, she suddenly remembered she'd heard someone on the porch after she had gone to bed. Perhaps she should have told the sheriff about that. Then she was glad that she hadn't. She was afraid that he might think of her as being some easily frightened person who jumped at every shadow and sound.

After writing some letters, Colleen tried to read a novel she had brought with her. But she couldn't keep her mind on the printed pages. She kept thinking about what had happened to her last night and the earlier ransacking of the kitchen.

So far the only people she had really talked to since arriving at Lake Topaz—except for the throng in the restaurant—were Linc Gordon, Scags Barnett, Jason Lewis, and Sheriff Denton. And, of course, that woman, Ivy Brooks, whom she had met so briefly. But somehow Colleen couldn't imagine any of them breaking into the cabin, scattering the sugar and flour and such, and then lying in wait for her on the porch the second night.

She certainly could scratch Sheriff Denton off her list of suspects. He would have no motive for doing any of these things to her.

Was the missing money that Scags Barnett had spoken about at the root of everything? Sheriff Denton didn't seem to put much credence in Scags's story. And it did sound somewhat farfetched in the bright daylight.

Still, Colleen mused, she had to take everything into consideration. A money motive certainly provided the best possible explanation for what had happened at the Scott cabin.

Linc arrived early, and Colleen was glad. She wanted to get away from the cabin for a while and enjoy the lovely scenery.

"Are you ready?" Linc said.

"Ready and eager," Colleen said. "I want to see as much of Lake Topaz as I can. Who knows? This may be the only time I'll ever be here."

Linc took her arm and led her to a small truck. "'Tain't fancy," he remarked, "but it will get us there and back."

"That's all that matters," Colleen replied.

As they drove away from the cabin, she had a million questions to ask about the road they were traveling, the houses they passed, and the scenery. Linc was up to answering everything. She found him to be a witty and intelligent guide. But about himself Linc was not forthcoming at all.

Still, she felt that he was far deeper than he allowed himself to appear on the surface.

At one point the conversation slowed somewhat.

Then Linc said, "About last night, at your cabin, did you get any look at whoever did that to you? I asked you that already. But I thought maybe you remembered something since then."

"No, I didn't," replied Colleen. "And I don't think that Jason Lewis saw anyone either."

"Jason Lewis!" Linc almost shouted. "What was he doing there?"

"He just happened to be passing by," Colleen said, startled at the animosity in Linc's voice. "Do you know him?"

"Let's just say I know about him. If I were you, I wouldn't have much to do with the guy."

Colleen didn't feel that this was the time or the place to talk about Jason Lewis; it was quite apparent that Linc Gordon cared very little for the man.

She was relieved when Linc turned off the main road and began to point out more scenes of interest to her.

He finally braked the truck and said, "Feel like hiking a bit?"

"Oh, sure. That's why I put on my jogging shoes," said Colleen as she hopped out of the truck.

Linc once again took her arm. His touch made her knees a bit wobbly, her stomach a bit queasy. Did it show?

Together they followed a trail through lush green foliage until they came to a wide expanse of sloping land.

"What are those?" asked Colleen, pointing to great holes in the ground that were being reclaimed by nature.

"Used to be iron mines at one time," Linc said with authority. "But they played out. Lots of them around this area."

Suddenly Colleen became aware of how isolated they were. She cast a quick glance at Linc, wondering if coming here was such a good idea after all. She hardly knew the man. What if she needed help?

Then she quickly cast this thought aside. Linc had been only kind and helpful to her from the beginning.

They found a shaded spot beneath a pine tree and Linc spread out a blanket. In his hamper Colleen found fried chicken, a crisp salad, and rolls spread generously with butter. There was also a thermos of coffee and some apples for dessert.

"You've thought of everything," Colleen said with enthusiasm. "This looks wonderful."

"I wanted it to be special," said Linc. "Better not judge until you've tried everything."

Colleen took a bite of the chicken, and it was delicious. "Scrumptious. Did you really fix all this?"

Linc pretended to be hurt by her remark. "That wounds me deeply. Of course, I prepared all this. When my mother died, my dad and I had to learn to make it on our own in the kitchen. So my father, a resourceful man, hired a chef to teach us how to cook."

Colleen wasn't sure whether Linc was telling the truth, but the food was excellent, so she didn't dispute what he had told her.

They ate and laughed and talked for hours. When it was time to go back to the cabin, Colleen felt it was entirely too soon.

"Did you enjoy yourself?" Linc asked as he easily guided the truck along the road's tortuous curves.

"Best time I've had in years. My congratulations to the chef."

They laughed companionably, and when they reached a turnout that overlooked the lake, Colleen could see the marina below them.

"I know what you're thinking," Linc said. His voice had lost all traces of humor. "That that must be where Jason Lewis works. You are right, it is his place. Only, as I told you, you'd be better off not having anything to do with the guy."

When Colleen looked at Linc questioningly, he changed his attitude and tone of voice. "Sorry, I guess I was speaking out of turn. I don't usually do that with people. I mean, talk about them when they aren't around to defend themselves."

When they arrived at the cabin, Linc refused her offer of coffee and told her he had some work to do at his cabin.

"Can I take a raincheck on that offer, though?" Linc asked, lifting his eyebrows in a pleading way.

"Anytime," said Colleen. "And thanks, Linc, I really enjoyed this afternoon."

"Same here," Linc said, then drove off.

Colleen stood there for a moment watching him. She wished she would get over that rubbery feeling she got in her knees even at the thought of Linc.

Turning, she noticed the garage door was open slightly and she thought she had closed it after driving her car in. To make certain that everything was all right, Colleen strolled over to the garage and opened the door wider. She walked toward her car and saw that something had been written in the dust that had accumulated on it during her trip to the lake: GO AWAY! YOU CAN BE HARMED HERE!

CHAPTER EIGHT

"How childish!" Colleen cried as she wiped away the message before she really thought of what she was doing. "Anybody who thinks I'm going to be driven away from Lake Topaz this way had better think again."

Furious at what she had read on her car, Colleen pivoted and walked out of the garage. She was closing the door when she became aware of someone watching her.

Turning her head, she saw Ivy Brooks standing not far away and looking at her with a puzzled expression.

"I thought I heard voices in the garage," Ivy said. "Is there someone else in there?"

Colleen felt a tinge of embarrassment because she had been caught talking to herself. Then she fought the redness in her cheeks by facing Ivy directly and saying, "It was just me. I found something in there that angered me. When I'm angry, sometimes I just speak right out, even if there isn't anyone around."

Ivy blinked her eyes as she moved cautiously forward. "Would I appear to be a prying neighbor if I asked what it was you found?"

Colleen couldn't find it in her heart to

think of Ivy Brooks as a prying busybody. The woman appeared to be genuinely concerned about her, and the look in her eyes was one of sympathy.

"It wasn't anything, really," Colleen said, then changed the subject. "If I fix a pot of coffee, would you like a cup?"

Ivy Brooks nodded. "That sounds like a great idea. It's just about time for a cup of coffee. There's a little chill in the air."

Colleen hadn't noticed this until Ivy mentioned it. She had been preoccupied with the message that had been written on her car and with thoughts of the afternoon that she had spent with Linc.

"I'd love to have you join me, Ivy," Colleen said, although something about the woman made her feel that she shouldn't address her so informally. But, as Colleen had found out, informality was the custom at Lake Topaz.

Ivy followed her inside the cabin and took a seat at the kitchen table while Colleen fixed the coffee.

When she brought two cups to the table, Ivy took hers and smiled. After she took a sip, she said, "Hits the spot. You make a very good cup of coffee."

Now that they were inside, Colleen was temporarily stumped as to what to say to the older woman. She was not usually without conversation, but Ivy was somewhat intimidating with her rather cold, hard eyes, though they sometimes softened when she smiled.

"Are you certain that everything was all right in the garage?" Ivy asked when the silence between the two of them became a palpable thing.

"As a matter of fact, I did find something there that upset me a bit."

"What was it?"

"I probably shouldn't make too much of it. Probably just somebody's idea of a practical joke."

It was evident that Ivy didn't intend to be put off. After a momentary deliberation, Colleen decided that she would tell the older woman.

"It was just after I came back from a picnic today. I noticed the garage door was slightly open, so I decided to check on my car. Anyway, someone had been in there. And whoever it was wrote something, a silly message, in the dust on the car."

Ivy shifted slightly in her chair and cocked her head. "Would you mind telling me what the message was? Or am I prying too much? Just tell me to mind my own business if I am."

Colleen noticed that the older woman was regarding her with the same unblinking stare that had caught her attention the time Ivy had first come by the cabin. Her wide mouth was spread in a smile or a grimace, Colleen couldn't make up her mind which.

"I don't recall the exact words," she finally said. "But it was a warning to me to leave the lake."

"A warning!" Ivy's eyes grew wide with surprise. "Are you going to do that? Leave the lake, I mean."

"Of course not. It was just the work of some crank or some jokester. I don't take it seriously. And, even if I did, it would certainly take more than a warning written in the dust on a car to frighten me into leaving."

Ivy took a sip of coffee and then brushed a strand of hair away from her eyes.

"Maybe it wasn't the work of a crank," she said. "Maybe you should take it seriously."

"You mean like what happened here in this very room? That I can take seriously. And what happened last night on the porch?"

Ivy shook her head. "I'm sorry, but I really don't follow what you are saying. What happened here in the kitchen? And what happened on the porch?"

"When I first arrived I found that a kitchen window had been left unlocked and someone had gained access to the cabin. Whoever it was got into the flour and sugar or salt and made a terrible mess. Sheriff Denton seemed to believe that it was just some vandal who was passing through. But after what happened last night, I don't think that he any longer believes it's a vandal."

Ivy listened quietly to all that Colleen said, that faint, almost amused smile still on her lips. At first this rather annoyed Colleen, but then she began to realize that this was just the way Ivy reacted to things. The smile was merely a mannerism.

"You say that something else happened

after the prowler got into the house?"

Colleen decided that as long as she had gone this far, she might as well tell Ivy everything. "When I arrived home last night, someone was waiting for me in the shadows of the porch. Whoever it was tossed a rug over my head and then gave me a shove. I was caught off guard and I fell down the stairs."

"I see," Ivy said, not once blinking her eyes as Colleen related the story. "It sounds to me as though someone doesn't want you staying here at the cabin."

"Well, that someone is not going to drive me away. I'm here to stay for the summer and that's it. And whoever is doing these things had better get used to the idea."

"You are a very determined person," Ivy said as she lifted the cup to her mouth.

"Stubborn would be more like it," Colleen said.

She was about to continue when there was a rapping at the front door.

Excusing herself, Colleen hurried across the living-room carpet and opened the door. She was surprised to see Jason Lewis standing there.

"You did say that it would be all right to drop in at any time, didn't you?" Jason remarked, a mocking smile touching his lips.

"If I didn't, I will now. How are you, Jason? Ivy Brooks and I are having coffee. Would you care to join us?"

Before Jason could answer, Ivy appeared at the door leading from the kitchen. "I must be going. There are a lot of things I have to do. I didn't really intend to stay this long."

"Oh, I'm sorry you have to go," said Colleen, not certain she meant what she was saying. "Do you know Mr. Lewis?"

Ivy dismissed him with a quick flick of her eyes. "We've met. Please excuse me."

With that, Ivy strode briskly across the carpet and out the front door. She didn't even say good-by. Oh, well, Colleen thought, that's just the way Ivy Brooks is.

"Dear Ivy," Jason said after the woman had gone. "We've never been able to hit it off. And she has such a charming younger sister."

Colleen didn't prompt Jason to go on, although she was becoming somewhat interested in Ivy Brooks and things that pertained to her.

"Tessa is her name," Jason continued. "Very pretty, but like a doe. If you know what I mean. Very much in the shadow of her older sister. Come to think of it, I haven't seen Tessa around for some time. Maybe she has mercifully left Lake Topaz."

"From the sound of that, you apparently don't care all that much for the lake."

Jason arched an eyebrow and his mouth turned upward in a cynical line. "You are very perceptive. I'm here for the money, and for that reason only. Frankly, I've never cared much for the beauty of the great outdoors. I'll leave that to someone like Lincoln Gordon. He's just the type who enjoys all this rustic, rural stuff."

Even though Jason's words were downbeat,

there was an amused twinkle in his eye that kept Colleen from disliking him and his observations on the lake and the countryside.

"If you don't like it here, why don't you leave?" Colleen asked as she started toward the kitchen to pour a cup of coffee for Jason.

"As I told you, there is a matter of money," he said as he followed her into the kitchen. Colleen poured him a cup and refilled hers, and Jason continued his conversation as they walked back to the living room and out to the front porch.

"The marina pays pretty well, and I do own a few cabins here that I rent. But I'm after the big bucks, enough to set me up in the style that I would very much like to become accustomed to."

Colleen took a seat, and Jason leaned against the wall of the cabin. She said, "Then you have no intention of staying here at Lake Topaz? You don't consider this place your home?"

Jason's laugh was bitter and somewhat evil. "Far from it. Even though I've only been there once, I'm all for living in New York. You can have all this peace and quiet. Don't tell me that you are content to be here? Not someone of your age."

Colleen held the cup in her hands. A faint, chill wind had arisen and the warmth from the hot coffee in the cup felt good.

"I'm not a big-city girl," she finally said. "Never have been and I doubt that I ever will be."

"That's just because you haven't met any-

one who could show you around in a big city.
I think that once you've been to New York,
you won't be content to come back to a one-
horse town like Lake Topaz."

"I rather doubt that I'll be traveling to
New York on a teacher's salary. Not for a
while, anyway."

Jason said, "All you have to do is find the
money that Mel Branson left here and you'll
be able to give up your job and really enjoy
life."

Colleen started to laugh, and then she saw
the serious expression on his face. "Don't tell
me that you actually believe that story about
Mel Branson and the missing money?"

"Why not? It hasn't been found."

"This place has probably been searched so
thoroughly that even a lost penny would
have been found. I don't believe that the man
left the stolen money here."

Jason's face seemed suddenly menacing.
His thick eyebrows came together and there
were frown lines etched on his forehead.
Then he smiled and the sinister look disappeared instantly. Colleen thought she had
just imagined it. Or perhaps it was the late-
afternoon lighting that had deceived her.

"Of course, you are right," Jason finally
said. "But it's rather interesting to speculate
that Mel Branson might have hidden the
money in a place in the cabin that nobody
would think of looking in. You've got to
admit that that might be possible."

"Anything is possible," Colleen said.

After that Jason changed the subject and

Colleen was glad. She was getting a little tired of hearing about the stolen money. As Jason spoke, she couldn't help but compare him to Lincoln Gordon. Jason's conversation always revolved around himself; he was obviously a very self-centered person. Linc, on the other hand, appeared to be more interested in other people and in things that didn't necessarily pertain to himself. Colleen checked herself before she carried the comparison further. After all, she was just here for the summer and she certainly had no intention of getting seriously involved with either Linc Gordon or Jason Lewis.

Jason finished his coffee and said he had better be running along. "That offer to take you for a ride on the lake still holds," he said as he moved toward the steps that led down from the porch.

"Thanks, Jason, I'd love to do that while I'm here."

"Take care while you're here, Colleen. Even though there are cabins scattered about, you are in a rather isolated spot. Anything can happen here in the woods."

It was a rather eerie way to say good night, and Colleen felt a slight shiver creep down her spine after Jason had walked away. Had that been a warning? she thought as she took her cup and Jason's and walked inside the cabin. Was it possible that Jason had been the person who had written the warning message on her car? She couldn't afford to dismiss anyone from her list of suspects.

Once she was inside the cabin, she closed

the door and instinctively bolted it. Outside she could see that darkness had begun to settle in. Colleen went from window to window, drawing the drapes and making certain that all the windows were locked.

Her thoughts went back to Jason Lewis and why he had actually shown up here tonight. She couldn't help but think that perhaps his interest in her might have been prompted by a deeper interest in the money that Mel Branson had stolen from the bank. After all, Jason had told her how much he needed and wanted money. He obviously did not like living here at Lake Topaz and might possibly stop at nothing to get the funds necessary to leave.

It was too bad, Colleen thought, because Jason Lewis could be very charming when he chose to be. And she couldn't help but flatter herself a little in thinking that he might be just a little bit interested in her personally.

"Well, if it wasn't Jason who wrote that message on my car, then who was it?" Colleen said aloud as she rinsed the cups out in the sink. Someone desperately wanted her to leave Lake Topaz. For the first time since she had arrived, Colleen wondered if she really had done the wise thing in accepting Millard Scott's offer to stay in this isolated place.

CHAPTER NINE

"Of course, you were right to come here," Colleen told herself out loud. "Don't let all this business get you down. Sooner or later whoever is playing these games is going to get tired and stop."

That seemed to help Colleen and she decided to fix something for supper. She really wasn't very hungry, but she did manage to heat up a bowl of soup that tasted good in the slightly chilled cabin.

After she had eaten, Colleen began to build a fire in the fireplace to take the chill off the cabin. Besides, she loved the smell of burning wood.

When the fire was going, she sat on the floor near the stone hearth and stared dreamily at the flames as they licked the crusty bark on the logs.

Colleen felt a sense of contentment as she sat there, and it was almost as though the flames were hypnotizing her. Then she forced herself to look away from the fire, and she got to her feet. There was still some coffee left in the pot, she knew. She walked into the kitchen and poured herself a cup before returning to the living room.

This time as she sat before the hearth, her mind began to drift from the flames to other things. She thought about the cabin and the kitchen. What a mess she had found in there that first night! It was difficult for Colleen to imagine anyone doing such a thing.

Then her mind drifted from thoughts of the kitchen to what had happened to her last night after Linc had brought her home.

Colleen closed her eyes and tried to imagine what the porch had looked like when she approached it after Linc had gone on his way. But she just couldn't force herself to see someone on the porch when in reality she hadn't. She had just felt a presence, not really seen anyone. Who could it have been? She was now certain that it was the same person who had vandalized the kitchen and written the warning message on her car.

She wondered how many people lived at Lake Topaz. One of them was the guilty party. But it hardly seemed likely that a stranger was doing all these things to her. Still, Colleen couldn't imagine how she had managed to incur someone's hatred in such a brief time. But apparently she had done just that.

Was that person Lincoln Gordon? Or Jason Lewis? Or Scags Barnett? These were the only people that she had really spent any length of time with since she had arrived at the lake. And, of course, there was Ivy Brooks.

Colleen shook her head. "I just don't know," she sighed as she lifted her cup of coffee to her lips. Scooting backward, she rested her back against the huge glass-topped coffee table and watched as the flames began to die down.

Colleen yawned after a while. She felt very tired. She left the cup on the mantel—she could take care of it in the morning—and got to her feet.

In the flickering, dying light cast by the flames in the fireplace, she stared at the portrait of Amy Scott. Colleen didn't know very much about art, but she felt that even though the painting was very lifelike, the artist, whoever he or she might be, was not top-notch.

She walked into the bedroom and got ready for bed. But when she slipped beneath the covers and fluffed up the pillow, she was suddenly wide awake. She reached for the paperback novel that was on the night stand, opening it to the place she had marked.

Before long Colleen found herself reading the same page over and over again. She put the book aside and switched off the lamp.

Lying there in the dark she could hear the faint crackling of the dying embers in the living room. It was a soothing sound, along with the faint, faraway sighing of the wind in the pine trees. Colleen felt her eyelids begin to grow heavy and she nestled down beneath the warm covers on the bed.

She drifted off to sleep, only to wake up about an hour later. She lay there wondering why she had awakened so suddenly. The sound of the fire crackling on the hearth had vanished, and the house was very quiet. Colleen was about to turn on her side and try to get back to sleep when she heard a sound, a sound of movement in the cabin. Then she heard it again.

Before she could think, she called out, "Who's there? Who's out there?"

Colleen sprang out of bed and grabbed her robe, quickly slipping it on. Then she felt on the nightstand, picked up a vase that stood there, and walked cautiously toward the living room. Before she entered, she felt along the wall until she found the light switch. With a quick movement of her hand, she switched on the light. For a moment it blinded her, and she stood there blinking until her eyes became accustomed to the brightness.

Glancing around the living room, she held the vase lightly in her hand. But there was nobody to be seen. Colleen couldn't help but give a sigh of relief.

Still, she decided to check the rest of the cabin, just to make certain. But she found nobody skulking around in any of the rooms or hiding in any of the closets.

All the same, Colleen sensed something was amiss and could not go back to bed. Instead she returned to the living room, this time looking around more carefully. Suddenly her disbelieving gaze was riveted to the wall above the fireplace. The place where the portrait of Amy Scott should have been was empty. Someone had taken the painting.

Colleen couldn't believe her eyes, and then

when she was in front of the fireplace, she touched the knotty pine wall as though she expected the painting to suddenly reappear.

A flashlight was lying in a small recess next to the fireplace, and Colleen snatched it up and ran to the front door. She flicked on the light, opened the door, and stepped boldly outside. It was dark and chilly on the porch, and she trailed the light around in the vain hope of maybe catching a glimpse of whoever might have taken the painting.

Deciding that it was no use, Colleen turned and hurried back into the cabin. She didn't hesitate as she moved to the telephone and dialed the number of Sheriff Denton. The phone rang several times before a somewhat sleepy-voiced sheriff answered.

"Sheriff Denton here."

"Sheriff, this is Colleen Evans. I'm sorry to wake you ... but this is urgent."

"That's all right. What's the problem?" Sheriff Denton was suddenly wide awake and alert.

"There's been a burglary here at the Scott cabin," Colleen blurted out. "An oil painting has been stolen."

"When did it happen?"

"Just a few minutes ago. Someone got into the cabin while I was sleeping and took it."

"I'll be right over," he said, then hung up.

Colleen walked to the couch and sat down. The cabin was suddenly an alien place to her. She listened intently for unfamiliar noises but heard none. Apparently whoever had been in the cabin was long gone.

But why take the portrait of Amy Scott? Even though it was quite pleasant it was certainly no masterpiece. And, Colleen thought, glancing around, just how did that person get into the cabin? She had locked everything before she went to bed.

Getting to her feet, Colleen quickly made the rounds of the windows and doors to be certain they were all locked. They were. She knew that would be the first question Sheriff Denton would ask when he arrived.

Just minutes later she heard a car pull up in front of the cabin.

Sheriff Denton's rapping was loud and urgent. Colleen hurriedly opened the door, and the officer came into the room.

"Now, what's this about a painting that's been stolen?"

"The one that was over the fireplace," Colleen said, gesturing.

Before the sheriff moved in that direction, he looked intently at Colleen and said, "Are you all right? You weren't harmed in any way?"

She shook her head. "No, but thanks for your concern. I was in bed sleeping. Something, some sound, woke me up. When I searched the cabin, I found that the canvas of Millard Scott's daughter had been stolen. It hung right over the fireplace."

Sheriff Denton moved quickly to the fireplace and looked around with a practiced eye. But Colleen knew he would find nothing in the way of clues. The person who had entered the cabin was very professional and very thorough.

"Was the painting the only thing that was taken?"

"I believe so," Colleen said. "Although I really didn't check everything. It was so obvious, the painting I mean, when it was missing."

"This may seem a foolish question, but I have to ask it. You didn't get a look at the person who did this, did you?"

Colleen shook her head. "By the time I got into the living room, whoever it was had gone. At first I thought I had been imagining things. Then, when I saw that the painting was gone, I knew that I hadn't imagined it."

"You did lock all the doors and windows before you went to bed?"

"Yes. And I rechecked them after I called you. They were all locked."

"Then we can only assume that whoever got in here has a key to the cabin."

Colleen wasn't prepared for that, and a gasp escaped her lips. "But that's terrible! Whoever has that key can come and go at will!"

"I'll send a locksmith over in the morning to change the lock if you like."

"Of course I would!" Colleen said, and then realized how that sounded. "And I thank you, Sheriff, for your consideration. I didn't know Lake Topaz had a locksmith."

"Not a regular one, but Scags Barnett can do the job. He's got the equipment."

"Scags Barnett!"

Sheriff Denton nodded. "Scags can do just about anything. He's a jack of all trades. Guess he's been just about everywhere in his life and done about everything."

At least she knew the man, Colleen thought, even if he did seem to be a strange old fellow.

"I'll look around outside," Sheriff Denton said. "Be back in a minute."

Colleen sat on the couch and thought about maybe rekindling the fire. But it was too late for that. She would be going to bed before long. In fact, Sheriff Denton returned almost immediately.

"As I thought, it is really too dark to make a thorough search. I'll come back in the morning. If you like, I can spend the night in my car watching the cabin to make certain that whoever did this doesn't come back."

"I wouldn't dream of having you do that. I'll be all right. I'll just put a chair against each door, and that should prevent anyone from getting in."

"If you think you'll be all right."

"I'm positive. I don't think our thief will be back. Whoever it was wanted the painting and got it."

"Looks that way. Well, if you do have any problems, call me right away. I won't be very far from the telephone."

"Thank you, Sheriff Denton," Colleen said as she walked him to the door. "I appreciate your getting here so quickly."

"That's my job," the sheriff said.

After he had gone, Colleen once again checked the locks and placed chairs against the front and back doors to prevent anyone from getting into the cabin.

When she got to her bedroom, she switched off the light and was about to go to bed when she happened to glance out the window. In the distance, toward Linc Gordon's cabin, she saw the flicker of a light, as though someone were moving through the heavy underbrush and the trees. Then the light disappeared.

Colleen stood there wondering if it had been Lincoln Gordon who had gotten into the cabin and stolen the picture. She shivered slightly as she moved toward the bed, a sinking sensation in the pit of her stomach.

Oh, Linc, she thought, was it you?

CHAPTER TEN

It was very difficult for Colleen to get to sleep after what she had seen. She got into bed and lay there staring at the darkened ceiling. Yet at least she no longer feared someone would break into the house. It was too late for that. Besides, she had a feeling that Sheriff Denton hadn't really gone home but had just driven a short distance away and was keeping an eye on the cabin.

Who had been in here while she slept? It could have been just about anyone. Someone she knew? Why would anyone take the portrait? To her it seemed of little value. But surely it would mean a great deal to Millard Scott. In the morning she would have to call him and tell him what had happened. In a way she dreaded doing that. It made it appear that she hadn't been doing her job of watching over the cabin. Yet she had been. What more could she have done?

Turning on her side, Colleen reviewed the possibilities. It might have been Lincoln Gordon, since he lived nearby. But, try as she might, Colleen just couldn't convince herself that it had been Linc. Anyway, she didn't want to think that Linc was capable of doing such a thing.

Then there was Jason Lewis. For some reason, it was far easier for Colleen to imagine Jason taking the canvas. Although Jason did have charm and she found that she liked him a great deal, there was something about him that didn't inspire trust.

Finally Colleen could not stay awake any longer and she closed her eyes.

When she opened them again, it was morning and the room was bright with the warm rays of the morning sun.

Getting dressed, Colleen went into the kitchen and fixed breakfast. She lingered over a cup of coffee, then returned to her bedroom to make the bed. She knew there really was no rush to get anything done, so she spent the morning just enjoying the cabin and puttering around.

Fairly early in the day Sheriff Denton had come by to look around outside the cabin for any clues that might help him find whoever had taken the painting.

"Nothing to report so far," the sheriff said before he left. "Whoever did this knows his way around the lake. But I'll keep looking and do some more checking around. I'll find this person yet."

Colleen was glad to be reassured that Sheriff Denton was doing the best he could to find whoever was doing these things to her. After he had gone, she decided she couldn't put off calling Millard Scott any longer. She got out the number he had given her before she left Arvin for Lake Topaz.

Colleen sat before the telephone for a moment or two before she dialed. She wanted to be in the right frame of mind when she talked to the man. At last she made the call.

"Mr. Scott? This is Colleen Evans."

"Colleen! Are you all right?"

"Oh, yes, I'm just fine," she said in as calm a tone of voice as she could muster. "I just thought I had better call you and tell you what's been going on here at the cabin."

"You arrived safe and sound, I take it?"

"Yes. It was a very pleasant trip. And I didn't have any trouble finding the cabin. But someone had been in here before I arrived. Apparently the kitchen window had been left unlocked, and someone got in that way."

"I don't like the sound of that. Are you sure you are all right?"

"Perfectly all right. Whoever got into the cabin concentrated on the kitchen—spilled some flour and sugar and stuff—but that's all cleaned up now."

Colleen thought she heard a sigh of relief, and then Millard said, "I'm sorry that that happened, Colleen. Maybe I forgot to lock that window when I was last there."

Colleen could no longer put off the real reason for her call. She would just have to come straight out with it.

"Last night someone got into the cabin and stole Amy's picture, Mr. Scott. That's the main reason for this call. I called Sheriff

Denton and he is checking on it."

"Amy's picture? But that was of no value," Millard Scott said. "It was a reasonably life-like portrait, but the artist was not a great talent. I don't know why anyone would want to take Amy's picture."

Colleen didn't know how to respond to that, so she didn't say anything. She waited until Millard Scott asked how the person got into the cabin, and she said, "Whoever it was must have a key to the cabin. Scags Barnett is coming over to change the locks on the doors."

"Good idea," Millard Scott said, and then there was a thoughtful pause at the other end of the connection. "Colleen, I wonder if it's such a good idea for you to be there at the cabin. Maybe I shouldn't have asked you to do that."

"Please don't worry about me, Mr. Scott. I'm not in the least frightened. Besides, Sheriff Denton is just a phone call away. And I've already met my neighbor, Lincoln Gordon, as well as some other people. I just thought you should be told what has been going on up here."

There was a faint sigh at the other end of the line, as though Millard Scott were trying to make a difficult decision. Finally he said, "Very well, Colleen. But please be careful while you are at the cabin. When you go to bed, be sure to lock both the doors and all the windows."

Colleen really didn't have to be reminded of that, but it was reassuring to know that

Millard Scott was thinking of her safety and well-being.

"I'll be very cautious," said Colleen. They chatted for a few more minutes before Millard Scott hung up.

Colleen felt that perhaps she should have told him about what had happened to her the night Linc, Scags, and she had gone to the restaurant for coffee. But she was afraid that he might have asked her to leave the cabin, and she just wasn't prepared to do that. She was determined to remain here at Lake Topaz regardless of all these mysterious and disturbing events.

Scags Barnett came by and changed the locks. He took an inordinately long time to do this, but Colleen didn't really mind. She enjoyed the old man's company, and he had story after fascinating story to tell her about Lake Topaz.

Nightfall took her by surprise; the day had gone so quickly. After she had fixed a light dinner, Sheriff Denton came by. He was becoming her most frequent visitor, she thought wryly. He hadn't made any progress in locating the painting, but there was a determination about him that assured Colleen that in time he would.

When she finally went to bed that night, Colleen lay there wondering why she hadn't seen Linc all day. She decided that he must have been busy with his work. She drifted off to sleep thinking of him.

In the morning her first thought was to be thankful she hadn't been awakened during the night. Perhaps the prowler was done prowling and wouldn't be returning to disturb her.

For the next few days Colleen just enjoyed the cabin. She went on long walks and nodded to her friendly neighbors. In the afternoons she swam in the lake and lay in the cool shade of the porch reading or just drowsing. It was all very relaxing, and Colleen found that she was not even thinking of the prowler who had given her such a bad time.

Sheriff Denton stopped by occasionally, but he had nothing new to report.

"But don't you worry, Miss Evans, I'll find that painting yet. Whoever took it is bound to slip up."

They were reassuring words, and Colleen really did believe he would eventually find the person who took the painting. But eventually could mean years.

The evenings went quickly by, and Colleen caught up on her sleep and did a great deal of the reading she had let slide during the school year. There were letters to write and telephone calls to make, so she was not without human contact.

On the afternoon of her tenth day at the lake, she finally felt a slight twinge of lonesomeness. The cabin was quiet, too quiet, and the wind blowing through the pines had a mournful sound to it.

She was sitting on the porch trying to concentrate on a book, but she found the task almost impossible. That was when she heard her name spoken, and she glanced up to see

Lincoln Gordon standing near the steps.

"You were out of it," Linc said in a friendly, good-natured way.

Colleen immediately felt that queasy, uneasy feeling in the pit of her stomach.

"Hi, Linc," she said, trying not to show the true extent of her enthusiasm at seeing her ruggedly handsome neighbor. "Haven't seen much of you lately. What have you been doing, hibernating?"

The warmth of Linc's chuckle was infectious, and Colleen did nothing to prevent an answering smile from touching her full lips.

"As a matter of fact, I've been out of town on import-export business. What's been happening around the lake since I've been gone? I hope things have been running smoothly."

Colleen suddenly remembered the light she had seen the night the picture had been stolen. The light that seemed to be moving in the direction of Lincoln Gordon's cabin. The smile froze on her lips, and she glanced away from Linc's penetrating gaze for fear that she might give away her thoughts.

"Tell you what," Linc said before she could reply. "Let me take you out to dinner tonight at the Bashful Bear. It's the best restaurant on the lake. Then you can fill me in on everything. I'll pick you up at six o'clock."

Without waiting for an answer, Linc was gone. Colleen glanced at her watch. She had a half hour to get ready. Linc certainly took her for granted! Oh, well, she was ready for some company and curious about the Bashful Bear.

At six o'clock Linc arrived. He looked very handsome in a corduroy jacket with a white shirt open at the throat.

Colleen was wearing a dress, and he said, "You look very lovely tonight. Just thought I would tell you that."

"No harm done," Colleen jested, and they both laughed and began to relax.

The Bashful Bear was a very nice restaurant albeit almost empty at this early time of evening. The hostess apparently recognized Linc, because she hurried right over and led them to a table by a wide window. Colleen thought the view was fantastic and said as much.

"Glad you like it. This is the best restaurant in these parts. The food is excellent. Try their filet mignon."

Colleen took Linc's word and ordered the steak. They also ordered red wine as a before-dinner drink and sipped from their glasses as they talked.

"Now, then, you were going to tell me all about the exciting events that have been going on here at the lake while I've been gone," Linc said as he put his glass down and leaned across the table.

"Oh, just the usual things," Colleen said. "Somebody got into the cabin and stole something. Nothing really exciting."

The smile on Linc's lips faded. "Are you joking?"

"Not in the least. It happened a few days ago. I was awakened by a noise, and when I went to discover its source, I found that

Amy's portrait had been stolen."

Linc's eyebrow slowly arched. His eyes narrowed as he glared at Colleen. "Did you happen to see the thief?"

Colleen shook her head. "Whoever it was took the painting while I was still in the bedroom."

Linc sighed. "Did you notify the authorities?"

"Yes, I called Sheriff Denton. He looked around but didn't find any clues. I really don't understand it. The painting certainly isn't especially expensive. There are several things of greater value in the cabin."

Linc was about to say something, but then his expression went through another change. His eyebrows drew together in a scowl and his full, sensuous lips narrowed in a cynical way.

"Well, well, if it isn't our new neighbor," came a masculine voice from behind Colleen, and she turned to see Jason Lewis approaching. "Don't get up, Linc."

"I didn't intend to," Linc retorted, his animosity undisguised.

Colleen glanced from Jason to Linc, and she could see that their dislike of one another was mutual.

CHAPTER ELEVEN

"Would you care to sit down?" Colleen asked, not really wanting Jason to join them for dinner since she was certain Linc wouldn't approve.

"Just for a moment," replied Jason as he took the empty chair next to Colleen. "I see you have finally found the one decent restaurant at the lake."

"You mean the Bashful Bear? It's quite a charming place. Linc suggested that we come here."

Jason glanced at Linc, but there was no friendliness in the look, although Linc was now doing his best to make the most of a delicate situation. "Now if I were taking you out, I would get away from Lake Topaz. There are a lot of fine places away from the lake. Topaz just doesn't make it, the way I see it."

"If you feel that strongly about the lake, why do you stay?" Linc asked, but Jason ignored the question.

"That offer to take you boating still goes, Colleen," said Jason as his mouth curled into a smirk. "Just name the day."

Colleen didn't want to anger Linc, but at the same time she didn't want to put Jason

97

off. "I'll think about it. Sheriff Denton didn't get in touch with you recently by any chance, did he?"

At the mention of the sheriff's name, one of Jason's thick eyebrows rose slightly. Colleen couldn't help but notice that he was suddenly visibly nervous.

"Sheriff Denton? Why would he be looking for me?"

"It's nothing," Colleen said, sorry that she had even brought up the subject.

"No, tell me. You've aroused my curiosity now."

Before she could speak, Linc said, "There was a robbery at the Scott cabin. Somebody stole the portrait of Amy. The one that hangs over the fireplace."

For an instant Linc and Jason's eyes clashed. It was Jason who looked away from Linc's unblinking stare.

"So what has that got to do with me? I didn't steal the picture. As a matter of fact, when you get down to it, the portrait doesn't do Amy justice. But I'll tell you one thing. If I didn't know better, I'd swear that you're Amy sitting here at this table, Colleen."

"The resemblance is that strong?" she said.

"You could pass for her twin sister."

"Only, Colleen isn't Amy," Linc said. "And that's all to the good."

There was a mocking chuckle from Jason. "That's right, you and Amy were going together for a while. What happened, Linc, did you strike out?"

Colleen was surprised at Linc's response.

He merely smiled. "Let's just say that it was the other way around. Only, I'm told that you wasted your charm on Millard Scott's daughter. All I can say is that she at least showed some good sense there."

Jason's eyes narrowed at Linc, and Colleen could see once again that there certainly was no love lost between the two men.

"I'll be going. Don't want to keep my guest waiting," Jason said, totally ignoring Linc. "Keep my offer in mind, Colleen. I'd love to get you out on the lake."

"I'll do that. Thanks for coming by to say hello."

Jason walked quickly away from their table and Colleen turned to look at Linc. Before she could say anything, she heard a laugh from across the room that sounded familiar. She turned her head to see Scags Barnett weaving his way through the tables, greeting everyone he met.

Arriving at their table, Scags wrinkled his nose and said, "Now here's a fine-looking couple. Are you going to buy me a cup of coffee?"

Scags could be irresistible when he chose, like an overgrown elf, and that was exactly how he appeared to Colleen right now.

"Sit down," Linc said, glancing at Colleen for confirmation of the invitation. She smiled her acceptance, and Scags seated himself at the table.

"Everything working all right at the cabin, young lady?" Scags asked. "No trouble with those locks?"

Colleen shook her head. "Everything is just

fine, Scags. You did a perfect job."

The waitress came by to bring Scags a cup of coffee and made a friendly comment to him. Everyone at Lake Topaz appeared to like the old man. Sometimes, though, when Colleen looked at Scags, she wondered if perhaps he was just putting on an act. But even as she thought this, she quickly put it out of her mind; she really had no justification for such an idea.

"What's this the sheriff was saying about a picture being stolen from your place?"

"That's right. That's why he asked you to change the locks. Someone evidently has a key to the cabin."

Scags shook his head and then pushed the glasses up on his nose. "What's happening to this place? Lake Topaz never had any trouble with thieves before. Except Mel Branson."

"It's beginning to sound as if it's someone who had it in for Colleen," Linc said, and Colleen turned her attention from Scags to the ruggedly handsome man sitting opposite her.

"Why me? I don't even know anyone up here."

Linc shrugged. "Maybe whoever is doing these things isn't from Lake Topaz. It might be someone who followed you here."

Colleen couldn't believe what she was hearing. "Oh, Linc, you must be joking."

Again Linc shrugged. "Well, who else could it be? After all, you said yourself that you didn't know anyone up here, so why would some stranger attack you and then steal that painting?"

"You're way off, Linc," Scags said. "I still think it's somebody looking for that money that's still hidden in the Scott cabin."

"Come off it, Scags," said Linc, a faintly mocking smile on his lips. "You really don't believe that that money is still in the cabin, do you? By this time someone would have found Mel Branson's hiding place."

"Don't you be so sure, Lincoln Gordon," admonished Scags before he took a quick sip from his cup. "Even if you don't believe me, I think that money is still hidden in the cabin. Branson hid it so good that nobody but himself will be able to find it."

"Let's change the subject," Linc finally said. "Tell us one of your whoppers about life here at Lake Topaz during the early days, Scags."

Scags didn't need any more prompting. He settled back in his chair and began to tell one story after another. Colleen didn't mind, for she found the old man's stories fresh and interesting. And he was a natural story-teller. As he spoke, she saw Linc signal to the waitress. When their food arrived, there was a steak for Scags. Colleen thought that very sweet and thoughtful of Linc.

"What's this?" Scags said. "I didn't order anything."

The waitress winked at Colleen. "Compliments of Mr. Gordon. So go ahead and eat it all, Scags. You don't eat right, anyway."

Scags looked at Linc, who just smiled and said, "The piper has to be paid. Dig in, Scags."

They all enjoyed the food, and Colleen didn't mind in the least that Scags Barnett had joined them. He kept them amused during the meal, and Linc proved to be an equally adept story-teller. Colleen found that she hadn't laughed so much in weeks.

The evening was turning out to be a very enjoyable one. Occasionally she glanced across the room and saw Jason Lewis staring at them. Finally he got to his feet, took the woman he had been dining with by the arm, and they left.

When Colleen turned her attention back to the table, she saw that Linc was watching her with a faint, almost amused, smile. She regretted that he didn't care for Jason. It would be far more pleasant if they could all be friends.

Scags launched into another story as the waitress brought their dessert, and Colleen quickly lost herself in the old man's words, the antagonism between Lincoln Gordon and Jason Lewis forgotten.

By the time Scags had finished, the restaurant was filling up. Most of the newcomers were not dining, however. They mingled with the customers in a spirit of camaraderie that was immediately apparent to Colleen.

"This happens just about every night at the Bashful Bear," Linc said, almost as though he were reading her mind. "This place is sort of the local malt shop, where the townspeople all gather to catch up on the latest gossip and goings-on around the lake."

People began to stop at their table, and Linc and Scags were quick to introduce Colleen to them. More than once a new acquaintance did a double take and mentioned her resemblance to Amy Scott.

There was a piano in one corner of the restaurant, and a woman began to play. She was very good. Scags told Colleen that she used to play professionally. Slowly the people in the restaurant began to gather around the piano. Colleen, Linc, and Scags joined the throng.

While the woman played familiar songs, they all sang along. It was a warm, friendly atmosphere and Colleen was glad that she had come along. Linc had a pleasant singing voice, while Scags was loud and just a little off-key. This off-key singing caused some good-natured ribbing from the other people, but Scags took it in stride.

The woman played whatever people called out. She seemed to know every song they could think of.

The owner of the restaurant brought out hot chocolate for everyone. People drifted away from the piano to drink their chocolate and talk.

"Having a good time?" Linc asked as the two of them sat down by the fireplace on one side.

"Very much. Wouldn't have missed all this for the world. Does this happen here every night?"

"Not that I know of. Oh, people do gather

here, but tonight is kind of unusual. Maybe word got out that you would be here."

Colleen studied Linc's face to see whether he was teasing her. It was difficult to tell with Linc. Sometimes she thought she had him figured out, and then the next minute he would be almost a stranger to her.

When Colleen glanced at her watch, she saw that it was almost eleven-thirty. "I'd better be going."

"Of course. I have to get up early in the morning myself," Linc said as he picked up his mug and drained the hot chocolate.

They made their way through the crowd of people, looking about for Scags, but he was nowhere to be seen.

They later walked briskly along the path that led to the Scott cabin. A pale moon shone and all around them shadows seemed to come alive. Colleen couldn't help but think of the last time she had walked home with Linc. That was the night someone had been waiting on the porch.

Linc walked her to the door, waiting until she was inside before he went on his way.

Once inside the cabin, Colleen gave a little sigh of relief. She was thankful that she had made it home all right. She listened for the sound of Linc's retreating footsteps, which quickly disappeared.

Going to her bedroom, she found herself humming a little tune, one of the songs that they had sung around the piano earlier that evening. Yes, she thought, it was a lot of fun and Linc is fun to be with.

Then she thought about Jason and how the two men definitely did not get along. She recalled that sometime during the evening Linc had referred to Jason as a "greedy opportunist."

She had immediately taken Jason's side since he wasn't there to defend himself. Linc had dropped the subject, but she could tell that he continued to seethe inwardly at the thought of Jason Lewis stopping by their table.

By the time Colleen got into bed, she found that she was yawning and fighting to stay awake. She knew that both the doors and all the windows were secured, so she just lay back and let sleep come to her.

Colleen hadn't been asleep very long when she was awakened by a sound. It was faint and almost muffled, but she was a light sleeper. Immediately she was wide awake. Sitting up in bed, she listened, her heart pounding in her chest. When the sound did not repeat itself, Colleen flung the covers back and got out of bed. She put on her robe and walked cautiously out of the bedroom. Flicking on the light in the hallway, she once again listened intently. Still there was no repeat of the noise that had awakened her.

As she went from room to room, she turned on the lights, half expecting someone to leap out at her. She was relieved when she found that she was alone in the cabin.

The noise, as she thought about it, really hadn't come from the house but from outside, on the porch. Picking up a poker from the fireplace, Colleen walked over to the front door. She turned on the light and then gently opened the door. A faint night chill entered the house and sent a quick shiver down her spine.

Colleen stepped outside and nearly tripped over something. Looking down, she recognized the familiar frame of Amy Scott's portrait.

Colleen picked up the picture. The night wind blew through the canvas, through the slash marks that had been made in the painting, gaping holes that had viciously disfigured the face of Amy Scott.

CHAPTER TWELVE

Colleen was momentarily stunned. Shivering, she held the mutilated painting in her hands, awestruck at the violence done to it.

Then her brain began to work again, and she realized that whoever had done this awful thing might still be lurking somewhere near the cabin.

Turning quickly, Colleen ran inside to close and bolt the door. She put the painting down on a chair as she hurried to the telephone. It must be very late, but she had to call the sheriff. He might still be able to catch whoever had done this terrible thing.

Sheriff Denton answered on the second ring; surprisingly he sounded wide awake.

"This is Colleen Evans, Sheriff," she said in a rush. "Sorry to bother you again. But you did tell me to call if anything happened."

"That's right. What's the problem?"

"It looks as if the person who stole the painting has brought it back. Only, it's been slashed horribly with a knife. I thought you should know right away."

"Are you all right? Surely no one got into the cabin this time?"

"No, I'm fine. I heard a noise and it woke

107

me. When I went outside, I found the painting on the porch."

"Don't go out again," Sheriff Denton said in a concerned voice. "I'll be right over. Keep all the doors and windows locked."

An unnecessary instruction, Colleen thought as she hung up. She sat quite still, staring at the slashed canvas. It was almost as though this were unreal, a dream from which she would awaken to find everything back to normal. She was acutely aware of noises outside the cabin—night noises: the wind and insects and the faraway barking of a dog. Common noises that suddenly seemed frightening and eerie.

When she heard the sounds of Sheriff Denton's car outside, Colleen breathed a sigh of relief.

She opened the door before he could knock. "You must be starting to dread hearing the phone ring," Colleen said in an apologetic tone.

"Not in the least. That's what I'm here for. As a matter of fact, things were getting pretty dull around here until you arrived. Oh, we had a car accident last summer. Tessa Brooks totaled Ivy's car. But nothing like what's been going on now."

"I hope that you don't think I brought all this with me from my hometown," Colleen said uneasily.

Sheriff Denton managed a friendly smile. "Of course I don't. Now let's have a look at that picture."

"It's over there on that chair," Colleen said

with a sweep of her hand.

The sheriff walked over to look at the damaged picture and slowly shook his head. "Hate to think of what was going through the mind of the person who did this."

"It's terrible."

"I don't suppose when you found the picture you caught sight of anyone?"

Colleen shook her head. "To tell the truth, I wasn't even paying much attention. I was too horrified at what had happened to the painting to think of finding out who left it on the porch."

"I'll take a look around outside. You stay here, okay?"

Colleen nodded. She hadn't intended to follow the sheriff outside. But she had gained reassurance since his arrival, and her terror at finding the damaged portrait was changing into a simmering anger.

What had been the point of this horrible act? Why would anyone sneak into the cabin, steal the painting, mutilate it, and then return it?

If the purpose was to frighten her into leaving Lake Topaz, then all the thief's trouble had been to no avail. It would take much more than these cheap scare tactics to drive her away. She had made a promise to Millard Scott, and she intended to keep that promise.

As she listened to Sheriff Denton moving about outside, Colleen once again thought about possible suspects. One by one names tumbled over in her mind.

First there was Jason Lewis. He was capable of almost anything, Colleen reflected. But how he could have a key to the cabin was something she couldn't figure out. And why he would do such a thing wasn't clear either. Yet now that she thought back on it, he had been there the night she had been pushed down the stairs of the cabin. Was he really just out for a walk, or had he pushed her and then come back to check up on his handiwork? Perhaps he couldn't wait to see whether he had given her a big enough fright to make her leave the lake.

After Jason Lewis, there was Linc Gordon. As much as Colleen did not want to put him on her list of suspects, she knew that she must. But she wondered, as she did about Jason, what motive Linc could possibly have. Was it that the stolen money might still be hidden in the cabin?

And what about Scags Barnett? Even though he appeared to be a local "character," she was sure he was really quite a shrewd person. For all his charm, could he be the one tormenting her?

At that moment Colleen's thoughts were interrupted by Sheriff Denton. "So far no luck. But I'll look around a bit more, if it won't bother you."

"It would bother me if you didn't look around. I'm going to put on a pot of coffee. Doesn't look as though there'll be much sleep tonight."

"No need for you to stay up," Sheriff Denton said. "This is just part of my job. I'm paid to do this."

"I couldn't sleep right now, anyway," said Colleen as the sheriff moved toward the door. "And doing something in the kitchen will get my mind off the painting and whoever brought it back."

"I see what you mean," Sheriff Denton said as he opened the front door and stepped outside.

After Colleen had put the coffee on, she went about the cabin turning on lights.

In the morning she would have to call Millard Scott to tell him the latest about the portrait of his daughter. She dreaded the call because she wasn't sure how Millard would react to the news. At the very least he would be upset, and he might even ask her to leave the cabin.

Colleen set about preparing her arguments against that alternative. She just couldn't leave now, not with all of these things unresolved. She had to stay to find out who was behind all that had happened to her since she had arrived at Lake Topaz.

Entering the living room, Colleen decided to build a small fire in the fireplace to take the chill off the room. While she did this she reflected on how excited and thrilled she had been at the idea of spending the summer here at the cabin. Now all of that excitement might end with the call to Millard Scott. But even if he told her she must leave, she had to make that phone call.

By this time the tantalizing aroma of the coffee perking in the kitchen drifted into the living room. It would have all been very cozy and pleasant had it not been for the painting which remained on the chair.

Colleen suddenly heard voices outside the cabin. They were masculine voices, and she walked quickly over to the door and flung it open.

"It's me, Linc," came his familiar tone. "Saw all the lights blazing and came over to find out what was going on. Then I ran into Sheriff Denton, and that really got me going!"

"Have you been home all night?" the sheriff asked him.

"No. I took Colleen out to the Bashful Bear for dinner. We stayed for several hours, and then I brought her home. After that I went to my cabin. Why?"

"It seems that picture of Amy Scott that disappeared has turned up again."

"Really!" said Linc with enthusiasm. "That's great."

"Not really," Sheriff Denton replied. "It's been damaged. And damaged very badly."

"That's too bad. But you don't think I had anything to do with that, do you, Sheriff?"

"Just checking on everybody and everything," said the sheriff in his official tone.

"Of course."

"Now that you're here, do you want some coffee?" Colleen asked Linc. "I'll bring you a cup, Sheriff, if you'd like one."

"Sounds great," said Linc, and Sheriff Denton nodded in agreement.

Linc followed Colleen into the cabin. She

gestured toward the painting but went on into the kitchen while Lincoln stayed in the living room to examine the mutilated picture.

When Colleen returned with a tray, she placed it on the coffee table and took a cup outside to Sheriff Denton. He accepted it with thanks.

Back inside, Colleen and Linc sipped their coffee as he began to ask her what had happened.

"I was tired and went right to bed," Colleen said. "I must have drifted off to sleep. Then I heard a noise and it awakened me. I got out of bed and looked around the house. All at once I realized that the noise had actually come from outside. That's when I opened the front door and found the picture."

Linc took a thoughtful sip from his cup and said, "I don't suppose you saw anybody."

Colleen responded with a quick shake of her head. "I was too busy looking at the picture to think about that. When I did, I got the heebie-jeebies and ran back inside the cabin."

Linc nodded. "A lot has happened to you since you arrived at the lake. First that mess in the kitchen, then what happened to you on the porch. Then the portrait gets stolen and slashed and returned. Quite a lot of events crammed into a short time."

"What are you trying to say, Linc?"

"Nothing. Except that it makes a person wonder."

"Wonder about what?"

"About why these things are happening. And to you. Lake Topaz is normally a very quiet place."

Colleen sighed. "You aren't going to tell me that I brought all this trouble with me from Arvin, are you, Linc? I think I've been told that before."

Linc chuckled. "Far be it from me to know the past or the future. Besides, I don't believe in such things. It's just that perhaps you should think again about continuing to stay here."

"You mean that, don't you?"

"Of course, I do. Doesn't it bother you that all these weird goings-on are taking place specifically around you?"

"What bothers me is that Millard Scott might not let me continue to stay here in his cabin."

They chatted for another half hour, and then Linc got to his feet.

"I'd better get back. Maybe the sheriff has found something by now."

Outside, the sheriff met the two of them, but he had nothing to report.

"I'll be back in the morning. And I'll question everyone who lives around here," said the sheriff as he began to walk toward his car.

"Thank you for all your help, Sheriff," Colleen called out, and he waved at her before he drove away.

"So you really are bent on staying," Linc said.

"Of course, I am. I don't frighten easily."

"Maybe that's not such a good thing," Linc said as he started to move away from the house. "Just be careful while you are here, Colleen. That's all I can say for now."

The darkness swallowed Linc up, and Colleen quickly turned and went inside. She bolted the door and leaned against it, thinking about Linc's parting words.

Moving toward the bedroom, Colleen thought this was the second time this evening that she had gotten ready for bed. The fire had died down on the hearth, and the cabin had a warmth to it that contrasted with her mood.

As she walked into the bedroom, the telephone suddenly rang. For a moment Colleen couldn't believe that it had rung. The noise shattered the quiet of the cabin, and Colleen walked back into the living room and picked up the instrument.

"Hello...hello..." she said into the mouthpiece.

For a few moments there was silence at the other end of the connection, but she could hear the sound of breathing.

Then a disguised voice said, "What you found tonight is just the beginning. You're in big trouble, big danger..."

A chill coursed down Colleen's spine. Finally she said, "Who is this? Who's calling?"

But the line went dead as the caller hung up.

CHAPTER THIRTEEN

"I can't believe this is happening," Colleen said as she slowly put the telephone down. She stood staring at the instrument as though it were alive and might strike out at her.

Who had it been? The voice was obviously disguised, so that Colleen could not even tell whether it had been a man or a woman. She walked quickly to the door but hesitated for a moment before she opened it. She stepped onto the porch and looked out into the darkness. There was a movement from some shrubbery nearby, and Sheriff Denton stepped out into the light coming through the doorway.

"Anything the matter, Miss Evans?" he asked as he moved closer to her. "As you can see, I've been sort of keeping guard here."

For a moment Colleen hesitated, not knowing whether to tell the sheriff about the call. Then she decided that he should know everything.

"I just received a threatening phone call," Colleen said, watching the muscular law officer move still closer to where she stood.

"You what?"

"Someone just called and told me the picture was just a start. There would be other things happening to me."

Sheriff Denton spoke very fast now. "I had a feeling I should come back here tonight. I'm glad I did. When did you get the call?"

"Just a few seconds ago. I was going to phone you just as soon as I could think properly. The call kind of threw me for a loop, though."

"I take it you weren't able to recognize the voice?" He was inside the cabin now.

Colleen nodded. "That's right. I couldn't even tell whether it was a man or woman. Whoever it was was obviously using a disguised voice—maybe talking with a handkerchief over the mouthpiece. Anyway, the voice was sort of muffled. Although what the person said was all too clear."

Sheriff Denton had been listening intently. "You weren't able to identify the voice by its tone or pitch? Nothing at all that we can go on?"

"I'm sorry, Sheriff Denton, but I was taken completely by surprise. It was so unexpected that I didn't really pay careful attention."

"That's too bad, but I can understand why you didn't. However, we now know for sure that somebody is definitely out to harm you, Miss Evans."

Colleen shivered slightly at these words. But she summoned up her courage. "I'm really not frightened. And I'm not about to pack my bags and steal quietly out of town. It will take more than a torn canvas and a childish phone call to make me do that."

"Good for you," said the sheriff. "I like a person with spunk. And don't worry, I'll keep a sharp eye on this place from now on. Have you any new ideas about who is behind all these things?"

Colleen slowly shook her head. "I really haven't met many people here at the lake. There's Linc Gordon, Jason Lewis, and Scags Barnett. Those are the three I can think of off the top of my head."

"If the suspects were limited to those three, I could make a good guess as to the guilty party. But I'll keep my opinion to myself until I have more evidence. Unfortunately, I don't think I can help you with that phone call, Miss Evans. I just wish that person would call while I'm here in the cabin so I can listen in."

Colleen walked with the sheriff to the door and then went back to bed.

This time she fell into a deep sleep from which she awoke feeling refreshed. Colleen lay there peacefully for a few minutes until the events of last night once again swept over her. Hastily she got out of bed and got dressed, all the while wondering who had made the threatening phone call to her.

Pouring herself a cup of coffee in the kitchen, she sat down and nibbled on a piece of toast.

Colleen tried to remember the voice. Had it been Lincoln Gordon? It was possible; he was so near at hand that he could keep a close watch on her actions if he chose.

Or had it had been Jason Lewis? If it had been Jason, she could very well imagine his doing it as a joke—even though it appeared to be a very mean, childish joke. But what reason would Jason Lewis have for wanting to harm her or frighten her into leaving the cabin? Unless it had something to do with the money that was supposedly hidden at the cabin, of course—Mel Branson's stolen money. That was the only motive that Colleen could come up with.

And if Scags Barnett had been the one, which she very much doubted, then once again the motivation would have to be the missing money. But after all these years, surely, if the money had ever been in the cabin, someone would have found it. Scags didn't believe that, though. He had said that he thought it was so well hidden that it still might be found.

Colleen glanced around at the kitchen as she thought about the missing money, wondering just where someone would hide it. The kitchen was out, she decided. There just wasn't any place to hide all that stolen money. It was more likely that the cash would be hidden in the living room. Perhaps in the fireplace. Mel Branson could have removed a few bricks, then replaced them after stashing away the money.

Colleen shook her head. "Now they've even got you believing the money is here," she said aloud and made a face.

When she had finished her coffee, she went

into her bedroom to make her bed and tidy up. Later, glancing through one of the front windows, she saw a movement outside. After careful scrutiny, she saw that it was the sheriff back at work. She wondered when he ever slept. But he looked as wide-awake and healthy as ever.

Colleen came out to the porch.

Sheriff Denton nodded to her and said, "I've been going over the place pretty thoroughly but haven't come up with anything. I'll have to give up for a few hours. I have a mound of paperwork I have to get at over at the office. But I'll be back as soon as I get that licked."

"I understand," Colleen said. "And I do thank you for all the time you've spent here. Sorry you haven't come up with anything."

"So am I," said the sheriff. "But I'm not easily discouraged. I'll find out who has been doing all these things yet."

"I'm sure you will," said Colleen with conviction. Sheriff Denton struck her as the sort of person who stuck to something until he found a solution.

"Hello, Sheriff," came a voice from the distance, and both Colleen and the sheriff turned to see Ivy Brooks walking toward them.

"Morning, Miss Brooks," Sheriff Denton said as he headed toward his car. "I'll be in touch with you, Miss Evans. And, remember, regardless of what I'm doing, you can always call in case something else happens."

"I'll remember."

"What was that all about?" Ivy asked as she came nearer to where Colleen was standing.

"Just some more problems I've been having."

As the sheriff's official car drove away, Ivy and Colleen watched it.

Then Ivy said, "You mean you've had more problems? Care to tell me what they are?"

Colleen studied Ivy Brooks's face, but there was no telling what went on inside the woman's mind behind that perpetual smile. It was a strange, mocking smile that sometimes made Colleen feel uncomfortable.

"Somebody got into the cabin and took a painting," Colleen said. "And then somebody —presumably the same person—brought it back. Only, the canvas was all slashed and cut up. It was a terrible, destructive thing for anyone to do."

Ivy had been listening with that faintly amused smile on her lips. Her eyelids narrowed somewhat as Colleen spoke, but she seemed to be not really listening to what Colleen was saying.

Still, when Colleen finished, Ivy shook her head and said, "Sounds to me as if someone has it in for you. Are you planning on staying around here after all that?"

"Of course, I am," Colleen said. "I don't frighten that easily."

"Well, if you ever need any help, just give me a call," Ivy said. "I'm in the book. And I don't live far from your cabin."

"Thanks, Ivy," Colleen said. "I'll remember

that. Only, I hope this is the last I'll hear from this weirdo."

Before Ivy could speak, the telephone rang inside the cabin. Colleen excused herself, and Ivy continued her walk. When Colleen picked up the telephone, she paused for a moment, remembering the eerie call that she had received only hours ago.

"Hello, who's there?" asked a familiar masculine voice that Colleen immediately recognized as belonging to Millard Scott. "Colleen, are you there?"

"Yes, Mr. Scott. I'm sorry. Is anything the matter?"

There was a faint laugh from the other end of the line. "No, indeed. As a matter of fact, business couldn't be better. But I was calling to find out how you were getting along. After what you told me about the missing picture, I wanted to check up on the way things were going there."

"Well, the painting did come back. Or, rather, someone brought it back. Only, I'm afraid it's been seriously damaged."

Colleen hated to tell Millard Scott this, but he was bound to find out sooner or later. Surprisingly, he didn't appear to be very disturbed by the news.

"Well, as I said before, the artist was not especially talented, and I was thinking of getting another portrait of Amy done, anyway. Maybe whoever did this was actually doing me a favor."

Colleen was relieved that he was taking it

so well. She had been so afraid he would ask her to leave.

"Have you called Sheriff Denton about this?" Millard Scott asked. "Of course, you did. That was a stupid question. Has he come up with anything?"

"Not so far. But I'm certain that he will. Sheriff Denton strikes me as very efficient and determined. Well, determined, anyhow."

Millard Scott agreed with that. Then he said, "Outside of the picture, how have things been going for you at the cabin?"

"I have to tell you that I received a phone call from some crank, telling me that I might be in trouble here. But I'm not worried about the call. The sheriff is going to keep an eye on the cabin."

"I don't think I like what I'm hearing. Colleen, do you think you're doing the right thing in staying there? I'm not at all sure that it's such a good idea now."

Colleen was quick to assure Millard Scott that he mustn't worry about her. "I'm all right. Really I am. And I don't worry at all. The sheriff is nearby, and I just don't think that whoever did this will try again. The cabin is too well watched now. Besides, the locks have been changed and the person who got in before can't possibly use the old key."

There was a faint sigh from the other end of the connection, and Colleen could tell that Millard Scott was wrestling with the idea of letting her remain at the cabin.

"If you're sure that you really want to stay

there, Colleen, I'll not ask you to leave. It's just that I feel responsible for you and don't want to see any harm come to you."

"I'll be fine, really I will, Mr. Scott."

"Very well. But you let me know if anything else happens at the cabin."

"I will. Oh, by the way, Mr. Scott, have you heard the story about some stolen money that is supposed to be hidden in the cabin? I met a man named Scags Barnett, and he was telling me about it."

Millard Scott made a doubting noise. "I don't put much stock in that rumor. Frankly, I don't think the money was ever at the lake, let alone the cabin."

They spoke for a few more minutes, then hung up. Colleen felt relieved that it was all over, that she had been able to tell him about the portrait and the phone call. At least she wouldn't have to look forward with dread to calling him.

There was a rap at the door. When Colleen opened it, Jason Lewis was standing there, looking very handsome in his designer jeans and a blue shirt open at the neck, revealing a mat of curly hair.

"Well, hello, Jason. What brings you here?"

Jason's lips curled in a mocking grin. "Now that's what I call getting right to the point."

Colleen couldn't help but smile at the way Jason looked at her. He was using his charm, and she knew full well that she was responding to that charm.

"It's not that I just happen to be in the neighborhood. I came over specifically to take

you for a ride on the lake. I won't take no for
an answer. You can't be that busy."

Colleen slowly shook her head. "No, I'm
not busy at all. And I'd love to go for a ride on
the lake. Should I change clothing?"

Jason looked her up and down, a little too
attentively, before he said, "You look just
perfect the way you are. Grab your purse and
we're off. And you can tell me everything
that's been happening to you since I last saw
you."

As Colleen went for her purse, she thought,
I wonder how much you know about what's
been happening to me since you last saw me,
Jason Lewis. And why are you so persistent
about getting me to go for ride on the lake?

For a moment Colleen had a presentiment
of evil; then she shook off that feeling as she
picked up her purse and walked over to
where Jason Lewis was waiting.

CHAPTER FOURTEEN

"Ready?" Jason said with a slight rising of his thick eyebrows. "You are a wonder. My car is just outside."

Colleen made certain that she had locked the front door before she headed down the path to Jason's car. He was quite gentlemanly and polite as he opened the car door for her.

As they drove along, Jason said, "You still haven't told me how things have been going for you. The last time we met was at the Bashful Bear, but Linc Gordon was cramping my style."

Colleen didn't want to go through all that again, so she quickly said, "Remember I told you that a painting had been stolen from the cabin?"

"That's right. A portrait of Amy Scott, wasn't it?"

Colleen nodded. "It was returned. But not in its original condition. The canvas had been slashed viciously."

As Jason Lewis listened to what Colleen was saying, not one muscle of his face twitched. She had no way of telling how the news was affecting him. Indeed, it might or might not have been news to him. His face was an inscrutable mask.

"I assume you didn't see this mysterious vandal."

"It was too dark, and I really didn't think of looking around until it was too late. But I called Sheriff Denton and he's working on the case. He feels certain he'll find out who's been doing all these things to me."

At these words Jason turned his eyes fully upon Colleen. He gazed at her from their brown depths with what she thought was compassion, almost regret. Then a slight, mocking smile tugged at the corners of his mouth, and the look was gone.

"Let us hope that the good sheriff finds his man or woman, as the case may be. Frankly, it sounds to me like the work of a practical joker."

"A practical joker!" Colleen said, aghast. "You must be kidding. Whoever mutilated that picture is a very sick person. And a very cruel one at that."

"Sorry," Jason said. "I didn't mean to offend you. Just trying to make light of a serious situation. What I don't understand is why you continue to stay in that place. It's becoming very evident that somebody doesn't want you there."

"I've been hearing that a lot lately. Apparently somebody doesn't know me very well. It will take more than a threatening phone call to drive me away from Lake Topaz."

Jason once again turned his attention from the road to Colleen. One eyebrow rose questioningly as he said, "You've had a threatening phone call?"

Colleen wished that she hadn't mentioned it. She thought she was beginning to sound like a skittery, easily frightened schoolgirl.

"Oh, it wasn't anything."

"Don't tell me that. You can't hold back on me now," Jason chided. "Tell me about the phone call. Who made it, and what was it about?"

Colleen sighed deeply. Then she studied Jason's profile, which was framed in soft sunlight. His jawline appeared tense, as if he were waiting for some disagreeable piece of news.

"Somebody called and told me that I could expect more of what had been happening at the cabin, that I was in big danger, big trouble. And I didn't recognize the voice. Whoever it was did a very good job of disguising it. It could have been either a man or a woman."

Jason's jaw seemed to relax. "And you still insist you're going to stay on at the cabin?"

"Of course, I am. Sheriff Denton is keeping a close watch on the place. I'm not going to be frightened away so easily."

By this time they had arrived at the marina. Jason opened the car door for Colleen and took her by the arm. "Come along. I'll show you what my business consists of."

It was a welcome change for Colleen. She

did not want to talk about the cabin any longer.

Jason took her through his business and proudly displayed his bait and tackle shop and a curio store that held very high-priced items. Colleen thought the merchandise was overpriced, in fact, but she held her tongue.

After all, it was Jason's store and he seemed to be proud of what he was showing her.

As they got into the boat that Jason had picked out for them, she felt a sudden uneasiness at going out on the lake with him. Anything might happen out there, and she really knew so very little about the man.

Jason seemed to sense her uneasiness. A slight smile touched his lips. "Don't get all tensed up. I'm an expert sailor. Nothing is going to happen to you out there."

"Whatever you say, Jason," Colleen managed to get out. "I trust you."

"Good. That makes me feel better," Jason said as he started up the engine.

The boat moved away from the shore, and Colleen cast a wistful look back as they moved out into the deep water.

It really was a beautiful day, and the sun sparkled on the blue lake. At first Colleen was slightly nervous at being there alone with Jason; then she felt herself beginning to relax as she began to enjoy the ride. Jason pointed out various points of interest, and he seemed to be enjoying the trip.

"When I'm out on the lake, I don't mind the

small-town atmosphere of Lake Topaz," he said. "It isn't a bad place to vacation, but I wouldn't want to live here all year round. Even though that's what I've been forced to do. But you just wait. I have a plan to get my hands on some big money. When I do, then it's good-by, Lake Topaz."

Colleen wondered if the big money he was speaking of was in any way connected with Mel Branson. She couldn't help but wonder if that was the reason Jason was so attentive to her. Maybe he was just using her to gain access to the cabin so that he could search it for the missing cash.

Colleen drove these suspicions from her mind. She wanted to enjoy the boat ride and Jason's companionship. What good, after all, did it do for her to be suspicious of everyone?

"What is that funny-looking rock formation over there?" Colleen asked, and Jason proceeded to explain what it was and how it got its name. She discovered that he could be quite knowledgeable about the surrounding countryside when he felt like it.

They had been out on the lake for about twenty minutes when Jason turned his attention from the scenery to Colleen.

"I just can't get over it."

"Over what?"

"The way that you're a dead ringer for Amy Scott. If I didn't know better, I'd swear she was sitting here in this boat, not you."

Colleen stared at Jason, who was looking at her with burning intensity. It made her uncomfortable to be scrutinized that way.

"You seem to know her pretty well."

Jason blinked and his gaze faltered. "Not as well as you may think. She wasn't an easy person to get to know. But I did take her out a few times while she was here last summer. Amy had a certain way about her. But we didn't part very good friends."

Colleen didn't say anything; she just sat there listening to what Jason had to say. She noticed that when he spoke of Amy, a certain hardness crept into his voice. It wasn't difficult for her to imagine Jason creeping into the Scott cabin and taking the painting of Amy.

Was there a pent-up anger inside Jason, an anger against Millard Scott's daughter, that would make him destroy her likeness captured on canvas? Once more Colleen felt very uneasy at being here on the lake, alone with Jason. In the distance she could hear the sound of a motor, but it was too far away to provide her with help if she needed it.

Jason had one hand on the steering mechanism, and he reached out with the other to secure it. Then he was free to move about the small boat. It was evident that he was used to the rocking motion of the craft, which Colleen wasn't.

"Yes, Amy Scott was an unusual person," he said as if he couldn't force himself to get off the subject of Millard Scott's daughter. "You know, your voice even sounds a bit like hers."

Colleen's uneasiness increased. She felt she had to do something, something to convince Jason she wasn't Millard's daughter. And no one else had thought their voices were at all similar!

"But I'm not Amy Scott," she finally said, sounding hoarse from the tension she had been feeling. "I'm Colleen Evans. And you and I are supposed to be enjoying ourselves on the lake."

One eyebrow rose menacingly on Jason's handsome face, and his mouth twisted into a wicked leer. He stood up and began to move toward Colleen. At that moment, the noise of the motor she had heard earlier shattered the silence between them. Jason and she both turned to watch the approaching boat. A lone person sat in it, and as it got closer, Colleen felt a great sense of relief to see that the person was Lincoln Gordon.

Linc pulled up alongside their boat, and Jason said with a snarl, "Just what are you doing here?"

Linc did not appear to be in the least intimidated by Jason. "There's a long-distance phone call for you, Lewis. I told your clerk that I'd come out and tell you. And I'll take Miss Evans off your hands while you go back to shore. No need for her to go back just because you have business."

Jason turned his head from Linc to Colleen. She certainly didn't want the two of them to begin another argument out here on the lake.

"You go along, Jason. I'll go with Linc. I really do appreciate your taking me out. We'll have to do it again soon."

That seemed to placate Jason, and the slight scowl that had appeared on his face vanished as he helped her board Linc's craft.

After he had gone, Linc said, "What were you doing out here with that guy? I don't trust him further than I can see him."

Colleen felt that she should defend Jason, since he wasn't there to defend himself. "Jason was very thoughtful. He just wanted to take me for a ride on the lake. It's very beautiful out here."

Linc glanced around. "I'll have to agree with you on that. Only, I don't think that Jason Lewis is the appropriate person to show you all this beauty. Sorry, Colleen, but I just don't like or trust the man. Hope you don't hold that against me."

It was such an appealing thing for Linc to say that Colleen found she couldn't be angry at him. Besides, she always felt unaccountably happy to be in his presence.

"Jason was comparing me to Amy Scott," she found herself saying.

At the mention of Amy's name, she observed an almost imperceptible twitch at the edge of Lincoln's mouth. It was almost as if she had struck a painful nerve.

"You might look like Amy, but you couldn't be her," Linc said in a low voice. "She isn't in the least like you."

"I don't know whether to consider that a

compliment or not," said Colleen as Linc began to guide the boat across the blue water.

When Linc didn't answer, she quickly changed the subject. They spoke of trivial things as Colleen lifted her hand to shield her eyes from the blazing sunlight. She decided she wouldn't tell Linc about the phone call she had received the night before. It all seemed a bad nightmare in the bright light of the sun. It was almost impossible to believe that last night had actually occurred.

Linc was beginning to relax now, and his smile was warm and tender. This was the Lincoln Gordon that never failed to make her feel weak in her knees. When he laughed at some silly remark she made, it was an infectious laugh that she couldn't help but join.

They skimmed the surface of the lake for about an hour, and then they decided that they had had enough for one day. As Linc began to guide the boat back to the marina, Colleen saw his wallet lying on the floor of the boat, and she reached down to pick it up for him. As she did so, a picture fell from the wallet and fluttered to the floor. Colleen reached down and picked up the photo. Before tucking it back into the wallet, she glanced at it. There was no mistaking Linc standing by his car. But it was a surprise to Colleen to see Amy Scott standing next to him.

Colleen looked up and saw that Linc was staring at her. For a moment she felt embarrassed, as if she had been caught snooping, but then she handed the wallet and the picture to Linc.

Tucking the photo back inside the wallet, Linc said, "Amy and I were just friends. I don't remember who took that picture or why I'm still carrying it around."

Colleen said nothing. But in her mind she too wondered why Lincoln Gordon was carrying the picture in his wallet.

CHAPTER FIFTEEN

Jason Lewis was nowhere to be seen when they got back to the marina. Once they were on land, Linc asked Colleen if she would like a cup of coffee. "They serve a pretty fair cup here at the marina."

"I think I could use one," was Colleen's reply as Lincoln took her by the arm.

Together they went to the small coffee shop inside the marina. Actually it was just a counter with a few stools scattered along its length. But Linc was right; the coffee was okay.

After they had been served second cups, Linc said, "Why don't I pick up some steaks and we can barbecue them at your place? There's a grill in the backyard."

"Sounds great to me," said Colleen. "I'll fix a salad and bake a couple of potatoes. You do come up with some good ideas."

"Thanks. They may not be totally original, but they're filling."

Suddenly they were both laughing. It was a good release, and Colleen found that she was beginning to forget what had happened on board Linc's boat and, for that matter, Jason's, too.

As if on cue, Jason appeared at the other end of the building. He was talking to a young, pretty girl, but when he saw Colleen and Linc, he left the girl standing alone and walked purposefully over to where they were sitting. Colleen glanced at Linc and saw that he was gripping the coffee cup so tightly that his knuckles were white.

"Well, Colleen, I see that you made it back in good shape," Jason said.

"Of course, she did," was Linc's surly reply. "I take good care of my women."

Before Jason could retort, Colleen said, "Thanks for taking me out for the ride, Jason. I really did enjoy it. And it was very thoughtful of you to spend some time with me."

Jason's anger quickly abated, and he smiled his warmest smile at her. "We will have to do it again sometime. There isn't one woman I've met who doesn't sooner or later fall under my spell. I'm not being conceited; it's just a matter of truth."

Colleen didn't like this arrogant side of Jason, but she managed a smile. Out of the corner of her eye she saw Linc's jawline tighten. She was relieved when Jason excused himself and went back to the girl he had been talking to.

After he had gone, Colleen picked up her cup and looked over the rim at Linc.

"I'm not going to say anything," Linc said with a low, dangerous tone to his voice. "As I said, the coffee here is fair—like everything else."

Colleen smiled at Linc and the tension quickly vanished. They sipped their coffee in silence for a few minutes, just looking around at the other people in the small coffee shop. Then Linc suggested they leave.

"That's fine with me," said Colleen. "I've had quite an exciting day so far. Can't wait to see what this evening will bring. Who said that things were dull here at Lake Topaz?"

"They were, up to a short time ago," came a voice from behind them. Colleen turned to see Sheriff Denton standing there. Apparently he was waiting for his order to be filled.

"Sheriff Denton, how are things going?" asked Linc in a good-natured way.

"Out doing my duty," was the sheriff's reply. He seemed to like Lincoln Gordon, and Linc apparently returned the feeling. "Just tracing some leads I've found. But for the moment, I have to take a little time out for food."

"You say you have some leads?" Colleen asked with wide-eyed interest.

The sheriff slowly shook his head. "Just some things I found at the cabin. Or, rather, outside the cabin. But don't get your hopes up too high, Miss Evans. They might turn out to be nothing."

From his noncommittal tone, Colleen deduced that he didn't want to disclose what these leads were.

And she certainly did not want to pursue the issue, especially since she wasn't all that sure that Linc Gordon wasn't in some way connected with what had been happening at the Scott cabin. But, in her heart, she prayed that he was just being a good neighbor and had no interest in harming her or in trying to find the missing money.

"I wish you all the luck in the world," said Colleen sincerely.

"If you need any help, Sheriff, you know where to find me," said Linc as he took Colleen's arm, and together they left the coffee shop.

Once outside, they walked toward Linc's car in the parking lot. When they were both seated, Colleen said, "I wonder just what the sheriff found that he's checking on."

Linc shrugged. "Who knows? Maybe a bent twig or a scrap of material from somebody's clothing. That's what they usually call leads. Anyway, that's what they call them in mystery novels."

"You're probably right. However, Sheriff Denton isn't the type of person to give away his secrets before he's come up with an answer. And, unfortunately, this isn't a novel."

Linc chuckled. "You are a realist, aren't you?"

"To a degree," replied Colleen. "Although I believe that I have a great feeling for romance, too."

Linc turned and gazed at her. "That's the part of you I like best."

Colleen could feel the color rise in her cheeks, and she quickly changed the subject. She just hoped that Lincoln hadn't seen the way she had blushed.

"How is Scags Barnett these days?" she asked.

"Scags?" Linc said, raising a curious eyebrow. "All right, I guess. I usually check on him two or three times a week to make certain he's all right and doesn't need anything."

Colleen thought this spoke well for Lincoln Gordon. Somehow she couldn't imagine Jason Lewis bothering with an elderly person. Then she felt guilty.

She hardly knew the owner of the marina, after all. Perhaps he had a heart of gold under all that arrogant materialism. At any rate, Colleen hoped so.

As they drove along the road, Colleen thought about the photo she had found in Linc's boat. Just how well did Linc know Millard Scott's daughter? Was there more to their relationship than he had told her? Perhaps the photo had something to do with the missing portrait from the cabin.

Wrapped up in these thoughts, Colleen unconsciously moved closer to the door on her side of the car. When she realized what she had done, she hoped Linc hadn't noticed. And apparently he hadn't.

Ahead of them the road curved; beyond the curve was a shortcut to the Scott cabin. In a way, Colleen would be glad to get back there. She needed some time to think, to evaluate her feelings.

"You really are deep in thought," said Linc, bringing Colleen back to reality.

"What did you say?"

"I just said that you were really tuned into something, and it wasn't my voice. Care to talk about what's on your mind? I know it's something. You've been unusually quiet since we left the coffee shop. Is it something I said?"

Colleen quickly shook her head. "No, it's nothing you said. I was just thinking. Nothing really all that important."

Linc appeared to accept what she said.

When they arrived at the cabin, he got out of the car and opened the door for Colleen. Then he walked to the front door with her; it was not really necessary, but Colleen certainly didn't mind. As she inserted her key in the lock, the telephone rang. She glanced at Linc, whose face was impassive.

"Come inside while I answer it, will you?" she said beseechingly, and he nodded.

She quickly opened the door and hurried to the telephone. As she picked it up, she was aware of an ice-cold feeling in the pit of her stomach. She said "Hello" and her voice didn't sound as if it belonged to her.

"Is this Colleen?" a woman's voice asked, and Colleen sighed.

"Yes, it is."

"Didn't sound like you at first. This is Ivy Brooks. I just thought I'd invite you over for a cup of coffee. That is, if you aren't busy. Thought the two of us could have a little chat and get better acquainted."

Colleen glanced at Linc and said, "Well, I could come over now, Ivy. For a short while. I do have a dinner engagement for the evening."

"Now is fine."

"Lincoln Gordon is here and I'm having dinner with him later," Colleen found herself saying for some reason.

"Linc knows where I live. He can bring you over. He's been here before."

"Let me ask him," Colleen said as she put a hand over the receiver. "It's Ivy Brooks. She wants me to come over for a while. Just for a short visit. She suggested you drop me off."

"Sure," said Linc with a slight nodding of his head. "I can take you over and then get our steaks for tonight. That way we kill two birds, so to speak."

Colleen thanked him and then turned her attention back to Ivy Brooks. "Linc will be happy to bring me over, Ivy. I'll see you in a few minutes."

"Fine. See you."

There was a click at the other end of the line, and Colleen hung up. She turned to face Linc. "You're sure you don't mind taking me over to Ivy's cabin?"

"Not in the least. Ivy's kind of a strange person, but I guess she's all right. She dominates Tessa."

"Tessa? The sister?"

"That's right. To tell you the truth, I think Tessa is terrified of Ivy. Don't know why. Ivy thinks the world of her sister. But I shouldn't be judgmental since I really don't know them all that well. Ready to go?"

"Let's go."

Ivy's cabin wasn't as far away as Colleen had imagined it to be. And Linc seemed to know the way very well.

When they arrived, he touched the brake and said, "I'll be back in about an hour. Will that give you enough time?"

"I don't plan to stay even that long," Colleen replied.

Linc got out and opened the door for her. As he did, Ivy emerged from her house. She waved a greeting to Linc and he waved back before getting into the car and driving away.

"Come on in, Amy," Ivy started to say, then quickly corrected herself. "I've brewed some tea for a change. Thought you might like a cup."

"That does sound good," Colleen answered as she followed Ivy into the cabin.

The interior was cozy enough, but Colleen got a strange, almost suffocating, feeling when she entered the place.

"You just take a seat here in the living room and I'll bring the tea," Ivy said in her dictatorial way.

Colleen was obedient, although she was beginning to think coming here wasn't such a good idea, after all.

Ivy didn't take long to bring in the tea, and it was surprisingly good. Ivy took a seat across the room from Colleen and began sipping her tea and making polite conversation.

All the while Colleen felt vaguely uncomfortable and resisted the impulse to glance at her wristwatch.

There was a movement from her right and

a young girl entered the room. She had thin and wispy shoulder-length hair. There was a haunted, almost frightened, look in her eyes, and the straight line of her mouth was an indication that she rarely smiled. When the girl saw Colleen, she gasped.

"Amy ... Amy, is that you?"

Colleen smiled at the girl and said, "No, I'm not Amy Scott. I'm Colleen Evans. You must be Tessa. I've heard a lot about you."

"You aren't Amy? Are you sure?"

"Yes, I'm quite sure. Although I've been told that I do resemble her very much. Will you have a cup of tea with us?"

Tessa glanced nervously from Colleen to Ivy and then quickly shook her head. "No, thank you. I'm going to my room."

Without another word, Ivy's sister pivoted and almost ran away. This made Colleen even more uneasy. Tessa could be very attractive, Colleen mused, if she did something with her hair and cleaned herself up.

"Don't pay any attention to Tessa," Ivy said. "She's a very shy person. Always has been. I have to take care of her. Not that I mind. She's all I have left of our family. They tell me I'm overprotective, but I pay no attention to unasked-for advice. Tessa is my life, and I'm going to take good care of her."

The rest of the hour seemed to drag by, and Colleen was thankful when she heard the sound of Linc's car braking in front of the house.

"That must be Lincoln now," said Colleen as she put her cup of cold tea aside. "I enjoyed our get-together, Ivy. And it's good to know that you don't live so far away that I can't walk over and visit you."

"I'd like that. Feel free to come any time," said Ivy as she walked Colleen to the door.

Linc met them at the head of the narrow path that led to the cabin. He exchanged a few words with Ivy, then took Colleen by the arm as they walked to his car.

Driving away, Linc said, "How was the visit?"

"I'm not sure," Colleen said. "All I know is that Ivy certainly is overprotective of her sister. But I guess that's none of my business."

"Maybe not. Ivy isn't an easy person to get to know."

Inwardly Colleen had to agree with Linc, and she tried to shake off the uncomfortable feeling she had been experiencing while at Ivy's home. She managed to do this by thinking about the evening ahead. But she had trouble forgetting the haunted look in Tessa's eyes.

CHAPTER SIXTEEN

"Steaks and all the trimmings are in those packages," said Linc with a nod of his head toward the backseat of the car.

"You think of everything!" Colleen said.

"I try to," Linc said. "Can't think of a better way to end the day than to have dinner with the loveliest woman on the lake."

Colleen felt the color beginning to rise in her cheeks. "Then you aren't planning on having dinner with me?

Linc cast a quick, inquisitive look at Colleen to be sure she was just joking. Then they both burst into laughter as they neared the Scott cabin. It was so easy and natural to relax with Lincoln. Yet there were times when she felt that he was holding something from her, that he had a secret he chose not to share with her. For all she knew, he might still be the person behind all that had happened to her since she had begun her summer vacation here at Lake Topaz.

Colleen didn't want to dwell on such thoughts, but she did want to be realistic about her relationship with Lincoln Gordon.

Linc braked the car and leaped out. He was at the other door before Colleen could even reach for the handle. Once she was out of the car, he grabbed the bags of groceries and followed her up the path to the cabin.

Glancing at the sky, Colleen saw that the blue was slowly being swallowed up by dark-gray clouds. "Looks as though we're in for a storm."

Linc glanced up and said, "It's not going to come down for a while. We have time to get the grill going and the steaks barbecued."

"All right. I forget that you're practically an expert," Colleen said with a slightly mocking tone to her voice.

"Practically is right," Linc replied as Colleen opened the door and they went inside.

Leading the way to the kitchen, Colleen stood aside as Linc put the bags of groceries on the table.

"I'll empty these if you'll get a fire going in the fireplace," Colleen said.

"Consider it done. And then I'll get those coals going on the grill."

Colleen bustled around the kitchen, putting the steaks out and the potatoes into the oven. She switched on the radio and lively music that matched their mood drifted through the cabin. In this atmosphere Colleen could almost forget about the strange things that had been happening to her since she had arrived at the lake. But then she walked into the living room and saw the slashed picture still resting on the chair.

This immediately reminded her that she had to be on her guard. She couldn't trust anyone, including Linc Gordon.

She could hear Linc outside, and once again she wondered if he could possibly wish her harm.

Colleen realized that if she dwelled on these thoughts, the entire evening would be ruined. Yet she admonished herself to be cautious. How little she actually knew about Lincoln Gordon! How little she knew about everyone on the lake.

Sighing, she returned to the kitchen. Moments later, fixing a green salad, Colleen heard voices outside, and she walked out the back door. She wasn't surprised to see Scags Barnett standing there, next to the grill, talking to Linc.

"Hello, Scags," Colleen said in a friendly fashion.

She was always pleased to see the old man, and she couldn't help but feel that at his age he might be just a little lonely.

"Top of the evening to you, Miss Evans," he said formally, but there was a twinkle in his eye. "Just passing by and saw Linc standing here, so I decided to jaw with him for a while."

"That's wonderful," said Colleen. "Why don't you join us for supper?"

Scags began to shake his head, but not very convincingly. "I couldn't do that. I mean, just barge in on you two. Truthfully, I was just taking a walk."

"Come on, Scags, stay," said Linc in his deep, baritone voice. "We have another steak. There'll be plenty for all. Right, Colleen?"

"Of course, there will. We'd love to have you eat with us, Scags."

"In that case, it's a deal," said the old man with what Colleen thought was a sigh. Scags was always welcome as far as she was concerned. And she knew that he and Linc hit it off. Besides, he was such a fantastic story-teller that he made the time spent with him extra special.

Almost as though Scags were reading her mind, he immediately launched into a tale about the early days at Lake Topaz. It was a humorous story, and both Colleen and Linc found themselves laughing as the old man spun his tale.

Colleen couldn't be sure, but she thought that perhaps Scags sometimes had a nip or two before he left his cabin. She had never seen him drink anything stronger than coffee, however.

When he finished his story, the steaks were almost done. Scags helped Colleen bring out a card table and some chairs. They decided to eat outdoors, even though there was a possibility that it might rain at any minute. In the far distance Colleen could faintly hear the sound of thunder.

"Good one coming this way," Scags said as he eased himself into one of the chairs. "Reminds me of the storm we had back in..."

And Scags was off on a new tale. Colleen brought the salad and potatoes out. Fortunately she had put several in to bake, and she and Linc enjoyed the story that Scags was spinning as they served dinner.

By the time Scags finished, they had begun to eat.

"Yes, sir, people drift all over the lake," he said. "You see them in one place and then another in the course of a day. Like when I saw you today, Colleen, on the other side of the lake."

Colleen glanced across the table at Scags. She suddenly really did believe that he took an occasional nip from a bottle. She hadn't been on the other side of the lake.

"I was on the lake, Scags," Colleen said. "But I never made it to the other side. You were mistaken."

Scags stared at her through his thick-lensed glasses, and his mouth made a sound before actual words came out of it. "No question about it. It was you I saw. Or anyway, I'm *almost* positive it was you."

Linc chuckled. "You'd better get those glasses changed, Scags. I was with Colleen most of the afternoon, and I can vouch for the fact that she wasn't on the far shore."

"Well..." Scags said, and he scratched his head. "Maybe I was mistaken. But someone as pretty as Miss Evans I would recognize anywhere."

After that they changed the subject, and Scags's apparent mistake was completely forgotten.

"That picture in there," Scags said, taking a big bite of his steak. "The one of the girl— Amy—what happened to it?"

Colleen shot a quick glance at Linc, who

seemed to transmit a message that it was all right for her to speak freely in front of the old man.

"That was stolen one night. I called Sheriff Denton and he did some checking around. Then whoever took it brought it back—returned it in that shocking condition."

"Sounds kind of sick to me," Scags said as he cut another chunk of meat from his steak. "You planning to keep on staying here?"

"Certainly I am," said Colleen defiantly. "That sort of vandalism isn't going to drive me away."

Scags munched on his food, then said, "Got a lot of spunk. Have to hand it to you, Colleen. Frankly, anyone else would pack up her things and slip quietly out of town."

"But I'm not just anyone else. And, besides, I'd miss you and your stories, Scags."

They all laughed at that, breaking the tension that had surfaced. For the rest of the meal they spoke in generalities. And Colleen was beginning to feel more relaxed than she had since she'd arrived at Lake Topaz.

For dessert she had fixed some fresh fruit and topped it with thick whipped cream. Colleen poured out some coffee as they attacked the dessert and enjoyed the remainder of the meal.

"Haven't had a good feed like that since I can't remember when," Scags said, pushing himself away from the table. "Next time you get up in my direction, I'll be the host. I fix a pretty mean pot of chili."

At the moment they were all too full of food

to appreciate the gesture, but Colleen managed to thank Scags for his offer.

Scags stayed for another hour or so. After minimal coaxing, he spun two or three more interesting stories. Then he stood up. "Better be going before that storm hits," he said, and soon he was swallowed by the night.

Linc insisted on helping with the dishes, and when that was done, they went to the front porch.

"Guess Scags had the right idea," Linc said. "I'd better be on my way, too. If you need me tonight, just give me a call. And take care of yourself, Colleen."

Like Scags, Linc quickly disappeared into the darkness. Colleen turned to go inside. As she did so, a flicker of a movement caught her eye. She stopped in her tracks and strained her eyes to see where that movement had come from. Yes, there had been a movement; something had reflected what light there was coming from the windows. Then, as she stood there, she saw the movement again. Someone was watching the house.

If she had thought about it, Colleen never would have been so bold. But she was angry. She charged off the porch in the direction she had seen the movement. It wasn't long before she found herself in darkness. But she knew that the window lights would guide her when she decided to return. Now all she could concentrate on was finding out who had been watching the cabin. Maybe, at last, she would come up with some answers.

Ahead of her, Colleen could faintly make out the figure of someone hurrying through the underbrush. Colleen was watching the figure so intensely she wasn't paying attention to where she was stepping. Suddenly her foot entangled itself in an exposed tree root, and she lost her balance and fell down.

There was a sudden pain in her ankle, but it went away as quickly as it had appeared. She massaged it for a few moments before getting to her feet. Then she waited to see if she had sprained her ankle, but decided she hadn't.

Peering ahead of her, Colleen found that she had lost sight of her quarry. Looking back in the direction from which she had come, Colleen also found that she had wandered farther than she had intended. She could no longer see the light from the cabin, and she felt a sense of disorientation.

"I could get lost very easily out here," she murmured to herself. "The wise thing for me to do is to head back in the direction I came from. It shouldn't be too hard to find the cabin."

Before she could move, something scampered across her feet, and she involuntarily let out a shriek. Calm down, she scolded herself. It was just some small night animal that's just as frightened of you as you are of it.

Colleen began to move in the direction she thought would take her to the cabin. As she moved cautiously along the tangled trail, she had the eerie feeling that she was being followed. Suddenly she was no longer the one doing the pursuing; she had become the pursued. Gooseflesh prickled on her arms and the back of her neck. She moved quickly along the trail.

The thunder had come closer now, and there was a distant flash of lightning. Colleen quickened her steps. The forest had that calmness that precedes a storm, and she was able to hear sounds acutely.

As she turned to glance over her shoulder, she thought she saw the silhouette of someone moving a short distance behind her. This was too much for Colleen, and she began to run, unmindful of the trail, her only thought to reach the safety of the cabin.

Just as she saw the lights from the windows, there was a blinding flash of lightning and an ear-splitting clap of thunder. Colleen sprinted for the cabin, dashed inside, and slammed the door behind her. Panting, she locked it, locking out the person who had been following her in the woods.

CHAPTER SEVENTEEN

Wind lashed at the windows, and Colleen heard its mournful sound as it swept down the chimney. She leaned against the door for support, slowly letting her breathing return to normal.

Who had been chasing her? She had no idea, but she was certain she had been pursued. At this very moment, whoever it was could be standing outside the door. Colleen swallowed hard and debated whether to call Lincoln. He had told her to call if she needed him.

She walked away from the door and headed for the telephone. She found the phone number Linc had given her and quickly dialed it. There was a faint buzz and a quick series of rings; then Colleen slowly put the phone down.

Linc obviously wasn't at home. But if he wasn't there, where was he? Had he been the one who had followed her in the woods? Certainly not, she thought. She had spotted the person just after Linc had gone toward his cabin. But it was quite possible that he had circled back . . .

Lincoln could very well be just outside that

door at this very moment. Colleen didn't want to believe this, but she had to consider all possibilities. After all, someone was persecuting her—it wasn't a phantom or a figment of her imagination.

At that moment there was a brilliant flash of lightning, followed by the inevitable roar of thunder. Colleen felt a surge of fear as the lights momentarily flickered. She thought they would go out. But they didn't, and she breathed a sigh of relief.

There was a sudden loud rapping at the door. Colleen froze in her tracks. Surely the person who had followed her in the woods wouldn't knock on her door! Colleen moved toward the door as the rapping continued.

She called out, "Who is it?"

"Me, Jason. Jason Lewis."

"Just a moment," Colleen said as she opened the door. "Come in, Jason."

The handsome man walked into the room and shook the rain from his clothing.

"Raining like cats and dogs out there," Jason said as Colleen closed the door and bolted it.

"How about a cup of coffee? I think there's still some left from supper."

"Sounds great to me," Jason said. "Thought you would never ask."

This was the same self-centered Jason Lewis that Colleen was accustomed to. She merely shook her head as she walked into the kitchen to fill two cups with hot, steaming coffee.

"Quite a storm we're having," Jason said

as she handed him a cup. "Only, it won't last for long. Should be over in no time."

Colleen took a seat on the couch. She said, "What brings you out on a stormy night like this?"

"Believe it or not, I was out for a walk. When the rain began, I was just passing your cabin. And I knew that you would enjoy my company for a while until the rain stopped."

Colleen couldn't help but smile at Jason's brash statement. It was so like him; he always believed that his charm would carry him in every situation. As Colleen looked at him, she began to compare him with Lincoln Gordon. Jason was self-centered, conceited, and basically without compassion for others. But she did have to admit he had a certain degree of charm that could blind a person to the real Jason Lewis.

Linc was just the opposite. He did care for people—look at the way he treated old Scags Barnett and, for that matter, herself. Of the two men, she certainly favored Lincoln Gordon.

"That was thoughtful of you," Colleen said, trying to sound as innocent as possible.

"Not at all. Have you been having a quiet evening at home?"

"Not really," she said, and then took a sip of the coffee. "Linc and I had dinner, and Scags Barnett joined us."

At the mention of Linc's name, Colleen saw Jason's lip curl in an unpleasant sneer. However, he didn't say anything, which was a relief to her.

"Before that I'd gone over to visit Ivy Brooks. Do you know her?"

Jason nodded. "We aren't the closest of friends. Although I wouldn't mind getting to know Tessa, her sister, a lot better. But that's out of the question with someone as domineering as Ivy Brooks. It just wouldn't be worth the effort."

"I met Tessa today. She seemed to be a nice person, although she appeared to be either terribly shy or frightened about something."

"So you noticed that, too. Well, after I leave here, I won't give a thought to Tessa Brooks and her heavy problems."

"Oh, are you planning on leaving Lake Topaz?"

"In the near future, yes," Jason replied. There was a slightly mocking tone to his voice. "I have a plan that I'm working on to raise some money. When that comes about, then it's good-by, Lake Topaz."

"I see," said Colleen as she lifted her cup again.

"And getting back to your evening, how long did our great and wonderful Lincoln Gordon honor your threshold?"

"He didn't stay very long after we ate. Scags left before him. Wanted to get home before the rain began. It was after Lincoln left that I saw somebody watching the cabin."

As Colleen said this, she studied Jason's face for a reaction. She noticed a slight drawing together of his eyebrows so a faint scowl appeared. Then he smiled.

"Somebody watching the cabin, you say?

Get a look at whoever it was this time?"

Colleen shook her head. "No, as usual, I didn't. It was too dark. But I was so angry I decided to go and find out who it might be."

"And did you? Go and look, I mean."

"Of course, I went. But I didn't get a chance to see who it was. I wandered too far from the cabin. Then I found that I wasn't the one who was doing the chasing. Whoever had been watching the house had started following me."

Jason listened intently to what Colleen was saying, although his features betrayed nothing of what he thought.

"I take it you got back to the cabin as fast as you could?"

"That's right. Besides, it was beginning to rain and I didn't want to be caught in the forest in a downpour."

"Of course not. Too bad you didn't get a good look at whoever was out there. Or maybe it's just as well you didn't."

Colleen raised her eyebrows. "Why do you say that?"

"Well, if you got a good look at who it was, you might be in danger here in the cabin. I'm sure that whoever is doing all these things to you wouldn't hesitate to use violence, if he or she knew that you were onto something."

It was a chilling thought, and Colleen reached for her cup of coffee. She held the cup in her hands to warm them. Jason was as impassive as ever, and she was beginning to wonder if perhaps he was the person who had been watching the cabin. Yet she tried to avoid this thought for fear that her face would reveal what was going on in her mind.

Jason, however, did not appear to be interested in what was going on in her mind. He was gazing across the room at the torn portrait of Amy Scott. It might have been just a trick of light, but Colleen thought she detected a faint sneer on his lips.

"Too bad that had to happen," Jason said. "It really wasn't such a terrible painting. As a matter of fact, it captured what Amy was like."

Colleen wondered if she were treading on dangerous ground when she asked, "How well did you know Amy, Jason?"

His attention strayed from the painting to Colleen. "As I told you, we were just acquaintances. Any acquaintance of Amy's meeting you for the first time would swear you were Amy. The resemblance is uncanny."

"I'm beginning to wonder if that resemblance isn't at the bottom of all this trouble."

"What do you mean?"

"Never mind," Colleen said, since she didn't feel up to discussing the portrait or Amy Scott any longer.

She was afraid that she might get too much information, and she was all alone in the cabin with Jason Lewis. If he had had anything to do with the theft and reappearance of the picture, she didn't want to know about it—at least not at this time.

Jason finished his coffee and got to his feet. "Looks as though our rain has stopped. So I'll be on my way. Thanks again for the coffee,

Colleen. And, of course, I know that you enjoyed my company. All the beautiful women do!"

Colleen walked to the door and opened it. She had had just about all of Jason Lewis that she needed for the evening.

Before he walked away into the night, he said, "Better lock your doors tonight, Colleen. That stalker might still be out there somewhere. Wouldn't want anything to happen to you."

Colleen stood there for a moment or two, watching Jason as he moved along the pathway. Somewhere, out in the damp forest, maybe that person was still watching the cabin. It seemed highly unlikely, but Colleen didn't want to take any chances. She pivoted and walked quickly back inside. Instinctively she locked the door behind her. Then she went from window to window, making certain that each one of them was locked. She checked the back door, too. As she did this, she thought about Lincoln Gordon and why he hadn't answered the telephone when she had called him. Had he been pursuing her? Had Jason appeared at just the right time and driven him away?

This hardly seemed likely. She found it difficult to believe that Jason Lewis was capable of putting a scare into Linc Gordon. If it came to a showdown, she would bet on Linc to come out the winner.

Her reverie was broken by the sudden jarring sound of the telephone. Cautiously she picked up the instrument.

"Colleen? This is Linc. I'm just checking to make sure that you're all right—that you survived the storm okay."

"Yes, I'm fine," Colleen said, not bothering to disguise her relief.

"You don't sound fine," Linc went on. "Are you sure you're okay? Has anything happened there at the cabin?"

Colleen quickly had to make a decision whether to tell Linc about being followed in the woods. Yes, she decided, she would—even though there was a remote possibility that Linc had been her pursuer.

"Well, yes, something did happen. After you left I thought I saw somebody watching the cabin. I know it was a foolish thing to do, but I went out to see who it was."

"You're right, that was a foolish thing to do. You might have been hurt!"

The words were reassuring, and she felt that familiar rubbery feeling in her knees.

"But I wasn't. Anyway, I fell, and when I got to my feet, I found that I had wandered too far from the cabin. On the way back, I knew that somebody was following me."

"I don't like this," Linc said. "Not at all. Did you happen to catch even a glimpse of this person?"

"Sorry, I didn't. It was just too dark. And when I was running back to the cabin, I was too frightened to try to see who might be chasing me. But, as you can hear, I'm all right now. And I've got both doors and the windows locked."

Linc listened patiently while she talked,

and she could almost see him in her mind's eye, his ruggedly handsome face so reassuring in its strength.

"You should have called me. I've been home ever since I left your place."

"But I did call you!" Colleen blurted out before she could think. "Only, you didn't answer the phone."

There was a thoughtful pause at the other end of the line. Then Linc said, "That must have been when I went to the garage to see if everything was secured there from the rain. Otherwise, I would have answered the phone."

Colleen pretended to accept this explanation, but she felt uneasy about it. It was too much of a coincidence, Linc having gone to the garage just at the moment she called.

She had just hung up the phone when there was a rough, loud pounding on the front door. Colleen caught her breath. She looked around the room for something to arm herself with when she went to the door. The person who had followed her might be right outside!

She picked up the poker from the hearth as she walked cautiously to the door.

CHAPTER EIGHTEEN

"Who is it?" Colleen called out in a strong voice, surprising herself.

As soon as she had said the words, she realized how ridiculous they were. The person who had been stalking her in the woods certainly wouldn't announce himself.

She was relieved when a familiar masculine voice said, "It's me. Sheriff Denton. I didn't wake you up, did I?"

Colleen unlocked the door and flung it open. "No, you didn't wake me up. I haven't gone to bed yet. So many things have been happening around here. Please come in."

The sheriff walked into the cabin and shook off beads of dampness that had fallen on him as he walked beneath the trees.

"You're right when you say that things are happening around here. I just came by to make certain that you're okay."

Colleen smiled at the sheriff, grateful for his concern. "I'm fine. Just had a slight scare earlier, but I'm fine now."

The sheriff took on his official look, and a slight scowl appeared on his face. "Just what was the scare?"

"I thought I saw somebody watching the

164

cabin from the woods. Right after Linc Gordon and Scags Barnett left. So I followed whoever it was. But I got the tables turned on me, and I ended up being the one followed."

Sheriff Denton listened attentively. "And you didn't recognize this person?"

Colleen shook her head.

"I don't suppose I need to tell you that what you did was quite foolish, not to mention dangerous."

"I know. I just didn't think. At the time I was so angry about everything that had been happening to me that I just decided to strike out on my own to see if I could find out who might be doing it all."

"You say that Linc Gordon and Scags Barnett were here with you tonight?"

"That's right. Linc and I were barbecuing some steaks, and Scags wandered in. We invited him to stay and have dinner with us. Is there something wrong with that, Sheriff?"

Sheriff Denton just shook his head slowly. "Nothing at all. In fact, it was very thoughtful of you to invite old Scags. You say that he and Linc left your cabin together?"

Colleen wondered why the law officer was suddenly so interested in Linc and Scags. "No, they didn't leave together. Scags left first and Linc stayed and helped me with the dishes. Then he went to his cabin. Why do you ask?"

"Just that I found Scags Barnett a short while ago in the woods. He had either fallen and hurt his head or been struck by someone.

He couldn't remember much."

"Oh," Colleen said, feeling sorry for the old man. "That's terrible. How badly was he hurt? Is there anything I can do to help him?"

"He'll be fine. I took him home. He wouldn't go to the hospital. But I made sure that he got into bed all right. I'm going to check in on him in the morning."

"That's really terrible. If someone hit him, do you think it might have been the same person I saw in the woods?"

"It's possible. I'm going to have a look in the woods now. It's probably too dark to come up with anything, but I'm going to take a flashlight and give it a try."

Colleen felt sorry for Scags, and she made a mental note to go to his cabin tomorrow to see if there was anything that she could do for the old man.

"Who do you think did that to Scags?" Colleen asked.

The sheriff was silent for a moment or two. Then he said, "As I said before, I have some ideas, but I don't want to make my move yet."

"Poor Scags. Living all alone. Somebody should look after him."

"Don't worry. There are plenty of neighbors who will look in on him. Scags is well-known in these parts. Although don't let me discourage you about going to see him. I think he's taken a liking to you. Anyway, I've heard him speak very well of you."

Those words gave Colleen a sense of guilt, since there had been times when she had been suspicious of Scags Barnett. Now that he had been injured, she regretted those thoughts.

"I went to see Ivy Brooks today," Colleen found herself saying in an effort to avoid talking about Scags. "And I met her sister Tessa."

Sheriff Denton nodded. "Quiet little thing, isn't she? Sort of walks in the shadow of her big sister. Can't tell you how Ivy carried on last summer when Tessa wrecked their car. You would have thought that Tessa was her child instead of her sister. Ivy is a peculiar person, no doubt of that. Haven't been able to get to know her well. Sort of keeps her distance from people."

That was the longest speech Colleen had ever heard from Sheriff Denton. He certainly had an incisive view of people. She idly wondered just what he thought of her, but she certainly wasn't going to ask. Instead she offered to pour him a cup of coffee to take with him when he went back outside, and he accepted.

Colleen went back into the kitchen, found some styrofoam cups, and filled one for him.

Accepting the cup, the sheriff thanked Colleen and said, "Be sure to lock the doors and windows after I leave."

"Don't worry. I've already done that. However, I don't believe that our friend will be back this evening. Something tells me that whoever is behind all this has gone back home for the night."

"I hope you're right," the sheriff said as he

walked over to the front door. "After I take a quick look around, I have to get back to the office. If you should need me, and I hope that you don't, just give me a call at the office."

"Thanks. I will," Colleen said. "But, like you, I hope I don't have to make that call!"

The sheriff left, and Colleen closed the door behind him. She locked it, then walked over to the couch and sat down. She couldn't help but think of Scags Barnett and what had happened to the old man. She toyed with the idea of calling him or even getting into her car and going to see him. Finally she decided to call Linc and let him know what had happened to his friend.

Linc answered on the second ring. "Colleen? Are you all right?"

"Yes, I'm fine. Sheriff Denton was just here, and I guess Scags isn't so fine."

"What are you talking about?"

"It appears that the sheriff found Scags in the woods. He had apparently either fallen and struck his head or somebody attacked him."

"You aren't joking, are you?"

"Of course not. I wouldn't joke about a thing like that."

"Sorry. It's just that it's such a shock. The last time I saw Scags was when he left your place after dinner."

Colleen switched the phone from one ear to the other. Linc seemed genuinely surprised at what had happened to Scags. That reassured her that he had had nothing to do with what happened to the old man.

"It must have happened just a little later. Probably before what happened to me."

"You mean when you were followed in the woods?"

"Right. Whoever was out there just might have attacked Scags. Caught him by surprise and struck him on the head."

"Does the sheriff have any proof that that's what happened?"

Colleen shook her head, then realized that Linc couldn't see her. "No, he doesn't. As a matter of fact, he's out in the woods right now looking around. Maybe he'll come up with something."

"It's possible that Scags simply fell. Even as well as he knows the trails in the woods, it could happen."

"I suppose you're right. He's been on my mind ever since the sheriff told me about him. Do you think maybe I should go over and check on him to see if he needs anything?"

"We'll both go," Linc said. "I'll drop by and pick you up. Besides, you don't know where he lives."

Linc hung up then, and Colleen waited patiently for the sound of his car. When she heard it, she opened the front door and stepped out on the porch. Linc waved to her from the driveway, and she turned and locked the door before leaving the cabin.

They discussed Scags all the way over to his cabin, which really wasn't as far away as Colleen had imagined it to be. Linc seemed very concerned about the old man. It was almost as though he regarded Scags as his own father. She liked this attribute in Linc. Still, between the bursts of conversation, Colleen mused on the significance of the fact that Linc hadn't answered the phone when she had called him earlier.

Could Linc have done this to Scags? Could he be so coldhearted as to attack Scags and then come running to his cabin to see how he was doing?

These thoughts were too terrible for Colleen to dwell on, so she dismissed them from her mind. She couldn't and wouldn't believe that Lincoln Gordon was that kind of monster.

When they arrived at the cabin, the door was opened by one of the waitresses that Colleen had seen at the Bashful Bear. She was an older woman, and she seemed to have taken Scags under her wing.

"How is Scags?" Linc asked as the woman greeted them.

"He's doing just fine. Got a nice-sized egg on his forehead, but other than that he's just as sassy as ever," the woman replied as she led them into the living room.

Scags was on a couch with a blanket covering him. He looked very little and old lying there, and Colleen felt her eyes well up with tears.

"Linc and Colleen," Scags said in a weak voice. "You didn't have to come out this late at night. But it's good to see you both again. Sorry about the way I look, but you give me a couple of days and I'll be my old self again."

"Of course, you will," Colleen said, patting his hand. "Do you need anything?"

Scags shook his head. "Bernice here, she just sort of took over. Bossy thing."

Bernice laughed. "And I intend to remain the boss. You get some sleep now, Scags. These two friends of yours can come back and see you tomorrow. Understand?"

Scags frowned slightly, but then he let a smile touch the corners of his mouth.

"Before we go, Scags," Linc said, "do you know what happened to you?"

Scags shook his head. "Don't know. Could have slipped and hit my head, or somebody could have conked me one. Maybe I'll be able to think more clearly tomorrow."

"That's right," Bernice said. "Tomorrow will be plenty of time for you to get your thinking straight."

Scags's eyes slowly began to close, and Linc took Colleen's arm as they tiptoed out of the living room. Saying good night to Bernice, who was going to spend the night in a chair by Scags's couch, they left the two of them alone.

On their way to the car, Linc tightened his grip on Colleen's arm, as though the gesture offered him a release of some kind.

They drove in silence back to the cabin, and Linc walked her to her door. Glancing around, Colleen couldn't see Sheriff Denton's car anywhere, so she assumed that he had returned to his office.

"I guess the sheriff is gone. I wonder if he came up with anything."

"We'll find out tomorrow," Linc said. "In the meantime, I think you should go inside and get some sleep. It's been a long day for you."

"You're right. I am rather tired," Colleen said. "I'm glad that Bernice is taking care of Scags."

"Yeah, he's in good hands. Good night. And be careful," Linc said. Then he walked to his car and drove away.

Colleen went inside and shut the door behind her. Someone's timing was perfect. No sooner had she closed the door than the phone rang.

Picking it up, Colleen was too tired even to care about who was calling.

She was surprised, however, to hear Tessa Brooks's voice. "Miss Evans, this is Tessa Brooks. I must see you and talk to you tonight—it's very urgent..."

"It's awfully late, Tessa. Isn't it something that can wait until tomorrow?"

Tessa's voice sounded frightened and almost hysterical. "No, no—it can't wait until then...I must see you tonight, while there's still time..."

Before Colleen could say anything, the line went dead. Tessa hadn't hung up—there was no sound whatsoever coming from the instrument. Colleen put it down, then walked over to where she had left the flashlight. Picking it up, she decided to go outside to see what had happened. Perhaps the storm had done something to the telephone wires.

Switching on the flashlight, she cautiously

moved around the outside of the cabin until she came to the area where the telephone line connected with the house. She trailed the light along the wire and was aghast to see that it had been cut! This had nothing to do with the storm.

Colleen ran back. She had the feeling as she fled that someone would suddenly reach out and grab her.

With relief she reached the front door, which stood open. Dashing inside, she shut the door, and then turned to lean against it. Someone was standing not far from her. It was someone she knew—someone whom she had visited only recently.

"Hello, Amy," said the cold, hard voice of Ivy Brooks.

CHAPTER NINETEEN

"Ivy! How did you get in?" Colleen asked as she stared at the woman, who seemed more hard than ever.

Ivy's mouth was twisted in an ugly, sinister grin that sent a quick chill racing down Colleen's spine.

"You left the door open," Ivy said in a very calm, even voice. "After I cut the telephone wire, I just waited until you went outside. Then I walked into the cabin."

Colleen stared at the woman. She wondered if she had heard correctly. "Surely you didn't cut the wire, did you?"

"Of course. How else was I to talk with you without our being disturbed?" Ivy said. "And I'm positive now that we won't be."

"I'm afraid I don't understand what you're saying, Ivy," Colleen said, meeting Ivy's unblinking eyes with a determination not to blink herself. "Why would you do such a thing?"

"Don't you know?" Ivy said as she raised an eyebrow. "Or are you just trying to be coy, Amy?"

Colleen was beginning to get angry. So much had happened today that it was begin-

ning to tell on her nerves. She didn't appreciate Ivy's little game.

"No, I don't know. I was just speaking to
Tessa and she wants to see me. Anyway, I
think that's what she said before you cut us
off. I think you owe me an explanation, Ivy."

"I don't owe you a thing. Right now I want
you to move away from that door, Amy."

"I'm not Amy Scott!" Colleen said in exas-
peration. As she did, she noticed the look of
cynical disbelief in Ivy's eyes. "You know who
I am. I'm Colleen Evans."

Ivy chuckled. It was an eerie, frightening
laugh, one that sent a chill racing down Colleen's back.

"Sure, I know. That's the name you've been
trying to fool me with, Amy. But it won't
work. I know that you are Amy Scott, the
very same Amy who was here last summer."

"But I'm not. Can't you see…" Colleen
didn't finish the sentence. She could tell by
the look in Ivy's eyes that the woman was
unbalanced.

"Move away from the door, Amy," Ivy said
as she slowly brought her hand out from behind her back. In it was a small pistol, and
she was aiming it directly at Colleen. "Do as
I say. I'm not afraid to use this gun if I have
to."

Colleen slowly moved away from the door.
She was afraid to make any sudden moves for
fear Ivy would squeeze the trigger.

Colleen's mind was racing, thinking desperately of some way to get out of the cabin.
She decided that perhaps her best hope would

be to keep Ivy talking. That way she might be able to make an escape.

"Was it you who broke into this place and scattered the flour and sugar and whatnot around when the cabin was empty?"

Ivy nodded. "Childish gesture, I must admit, but it did give you a bit of a fright, I hope."

Ivy was speaking with such venom that Colleen had to fight to suppress any outward expression of the fear she felt.

"How did you get in?"

"I had a key to the cabin. You were so careless last summer, Amy. Always leaving your things lying around. I had a duplicate key made and returned the original to your key ring. You didn't even notice the keys were gone. All I had to do was just come in here and have a little fun."

Ivy laughed then. It was a maniacal laugh, full of hatred and evil. Before Colleen's eyes the woman changed. There was little doubt in her mind that Ivy was insane.

"Then it was also you who hid on the porch the night I came back from the restaurant. And then you tossed that rug over me and pushed me down the stairs."

Ivy nodded slowly. "You are a very bright girl, Amy. Bright and spoiled and used to having your own way. Not caring whom you stepped on and how you damaged other people's things."

Colleen knew she had to keep Ivy talking or she might do something with the weapon she was holding in her hand.

"Was it you who took the painting?"

Ivy glanced at the damaged canvas, then back at Colleen. "You were sound asleep that night when I came in here. It would have been so easy for me to have done something to you. But I decided to take the painting. I wasn't ready yet to let you off the hook so easily. Then I brought the picture back and walked around on the porch so that you would wake up and find it."

"You wrote that message on the car, too, didn't you?"

Again Ivy nodded. "At first I thought I'd just frighten you away. But you didn't frighten as easily as I hoped. So I decided that more serious measures were called for."

Colleen didn't want to ask Ivy why she had done all these things. She felt that the minute Ivy answered that question, her chances for survival would be very slim indeed.

"What about Scags Barnett?"

"What about him?"

"Did you strike him on the head while he was walking home from here?"

Ivy seemed momentarily perplexed; then she said, "I've got nothing against that old man. I didn't hit him. I haven't been near your place until now."

"But I saw you—or somebody—in the woods, and I followed. It wasn't you?"

"No, it wasn't me. Haven't any idea who it was."

Colleen saw that Ivy was beginning to get nervous. She still held the gun firmly in her hand, pointed at Colleen. If only she could think of some way to distract Ivy and then make a run for it.

"You know you could put that gun down and walk out of here," Colleen said. "You don't really want to hurt me, do you, Ivy?"

The gun, which for a moment had wavered in the woman's hand, suddenly ceased its movement as Ivy gained control over it.

"Of course, I do. That's why I'm here. Only, this time I'm going to make a good job of it. Hurt you just the way you hurt Tessa."

"Tessa?" Colleen said in a hushed voice. "What has she got to do with all this?"

"Don't play the innocent with me, Amy Scott," Ivy said in a loud voice. "You know what you did to her. Last summer you did it. I swore then that I would get even with you. You think that you can control everything and everyone here at the lake. Just like your father. You think that having money gives you special privileges."

Colleen realized that she was getting dangerously close to finding out why Ivy had been tormenting her. But it was too late to turn back now. And, she was certain, Ivy wouldn't turn back.

"But what did I do?" Colleen asked, temporarily assuming the persona of Amy Scott.

Ivy's laugh was chilling. Her eyes were blazing now with hatred and malice. It was all that Colleen could do just to look at the woman. She moved slightly, and her leg struck the rack that held the fire irons. This was as far back as Colleen could move. Her mind was whirling as she tried to think of some way that she might escape from this madwoman.

She hadn't locked the front door, but Ivy stood between it and herself. If she could somehow maneuver Ivy around to the other side of the room, perhaps she could make a break for it. A sudden move might throw Ivy off guard.

But Colleen decided it was too chancy to attempt. She had no idea what sort of marksman Ivy was with the gun. She couldn't take the risk.

As they stood facing each other, Colleen thought she saw the knob on the front door begin to turn. She silently prayed that it would be someone to help her. She quickly turned her attention back to Ivy for fear the woman might look at the door.

"For the last time, Ivy, I'm asking you to put down that gun and not do anything foolish," Colleen said with more conviction than she actually felt.

"Foolish! I doubt that what I came here to do could be called foolish, Amy Scott," Ivy said in a loud, angry voice.

At that moment the front door opened and someone walked into the room. Colleen couldn't help but gasp when she saw who it was. She could have been looking into a mirror, seeing her own reflection—moving, breathing, alive. It was Amy Scott.

Ivy heard the movement, and she turned to look at the door. Ivy gasped too when she saw Amy Scott.

Colleen was the first one to regain her

senses, and she reached behind herself and grabbed one of the fireplace implements. It turned out to be a small shovel. Ivy at that moment looked at her, then shifted her dazed and bewildered eyes toward the real Amy Scott.

Seizing the opportunity that presented itself, Colleen lifted the shovel and brought it down on Ivy's hand, the one that held the weapon. With a cry of pain, Ivy dropped the gun; then she whirled to face Colleen.

The front door was flung open wider, and Lincoln Gordon rushed into the room and grabbed Ivy Brooks, who was about to attack Colleen with her strong hands.

"Call Sheriff Denton, sweetheart," Linc said as he pinned the raging Ivy's hands behind her back. "I've patched up the phone line. Checked it when I couldn't call you."

Ivy struggled violently with Linc for a few moments as Colleen made the call to the sheriff. Then Ivy seemed to wilt; all the energy left her, and she sagged against Linc, who took her to the couch where he eased her down.

"Oh, Linc, it was Ivy who was behind all these things," Colleen said, still remembering that Linc had called her sweetheart when he'd told her to call the sheriff.

"Why did she do it?" Linc asked as he walked over and picked up the gun. As he did this, he seemed to notice Amy for the first time. "Amy! What are you doing here?"

"Dad told me what was going on here, and I decided to come up and find out for myself," the daughter of Millard Scott said. "I arrived yesterday and stayed with some friends. I thought I would watch the cabin and see who might be doing these things to Miss Evans."

"Then it was you I saw in the woods, not Ivy," said Colleen.

"That's right. You started to follow me, so I had to make tracks. When you fell, I came back to see if you were all right."

"It looks as though Scags simply fell and struck his head," Colleen said. "But I still don't understand why Ivy has been doing all these things to me."

"I think I can explain that," a woman's voice said.

They all turned to see Tessa Brooks standing in the doorway.

"It was because of me, little Tessa. That's why I called you tonight, Miss Evans. I wanted to talk to you about Ivy."

Colleen glanced from Tessa to Ivy, but the older woman was just sitting there, lost in her own world.

"Ivy has always been overprotective of me," Tessa said. "All my life, ever since our parents died, she has dominated me. I know that she thought she was doing the right thing, but it was suffocating me. She grew worse each year, beginning to imagine all sorts of things. Then last summer I borrowed her car and had an accident. When Ivy came to help me, Amy Scott happened to be passing by. For some reason, Ivy got it in her head that Amy had forced me off the road and caused the accident. She just wouldn't allow herself to believe that it was all my fault."

"Then it was Ivy who did all these things to Colleen," Linc said. "Thinking that she was really Amy Scott."

"That's right," Tessa said. "It was only tonight when I found a piece of the canvas that she had slashed that I put it all together. I'm very sorry, Miss Evans."

It wasn't long before Sheriff Denton arrived and took Ivy Brooks away with him. Tessa went with her, and Colleen couldn't help but feel sad at what had happened to the unfortunate woman.

"She'll probably be sent away for mental help," Amy Scott said after they had gone. "Sorry that you had to go through all this, Colleen."

"I wasn't hurt, not really," said Colleen. "It could have been worse. I suppose you'll be taking over the cabin for the rest of the summer?"

Amy Scott shook her head. "I just slipped away to come up here. I wouldn't dream of barging in on your vacation. I just hope that you have a pleasant summer from now on."

"I intend to," said Colleen. "And I want to thank you for coming in when you did. Otherwise, I don't know what Ivy would have done to me."

"Things did work out for the best," said Amy with a smile. "I'd better be going now. I want to get some sleep before I leave tomorrow."

Amy shook hands with Colleen and did the

same with Linc, which surprised Colleen. After Millard Scott's daughter had gone, Colleen said, "I guess you and Amy were just good friends, after all."

"Did you ever doubt me?" Linc said as he reached out and took her in his arms. Before Colleen could speak, Linc placed a gentle yet thrilling kiss on her lips.

"What was that for?" asked Colleen as she gazed up into Linc's eyes.

"Just a reminder of what lies ahead of you for the summer," he said. "And not just for this summer, but for many summers to come."

"You aren't suggesting that I come back here every summer, are you, Lincoln Gordon?"

"No," Linc said, and Colleen's heart momentarily sank. "I'm suggesting that you stay with me for all the seasons—as my wife, of course. That is, if you will have me."

In answer Colleen stood on her tiptoes and ardently kissed Linc. "Does that answer the question for you?" she said.

"Better than a thousand words," was his reply. And then he pulled her close, kissing her several times more for good measure.